Rick

Ingram Brothers #3

ROZ LEE

Ingram
Brothers #3
PICK
USA TODAY BESTSELLING AUT
ROZLEE

DEDICATION

To all those brave souls who find the courage to love.

ACKNOWLEDGMENTS

I'd like to thank my family for standing by me in my crazy pursuit of literary fame, if not fortune. Your support gives me the courage to put words on paper and send them out into the world, as imperfect as they may be.

I'd be remiss if I didn't thank my editor, Laura Garland, for making it seem like I know what I'm doing when I'm nothing more than a storyteller.

To those of you who read my stories, I keep you close to my heart every day. Thank you. Thank you. Thank you.

Roz Lee

PROLOGUE

Six years ago…

Rick thanked the Uber driver then stepped out onto the sidewalk in front of the bar. He'd been here a couple of times. It had become his go-to place the night before shipping out. The place had a good reputation for discretion and safety. And, it was clear across town from the military base he called home when he wasn't in some hellhole overseas. The Marines had been good to him, providing him with the discipline and structure he'd needed in his life. He wasn't ready to make the Corps his career, but he wasn't ready to give it up, either, though he didn't know how much longer he could hide his sexual orientation. He wasn't keen on coming out to his brothers, and he sure as hell wasn't going to tell the Corps. There was some shit better kept in the closet. Preferring dick to pussy was one of them.

He'd be shipping out Monday for a year-long deployment to Iraq, his second deployment to the war-torn region. In honor of the occasion, his entire unit had been given the weekend off to say their goodbyes and to get their shit together. Those with families nearby had gone home. The rest had hightailed it off base to the nearest watering hole to get shitfaced and find some pussy.

This place guaranteed he could have a couple of beers and not be hit on by sword bunnies—desperate women with dreams of a military wedding. They'd settle for becoming some Marine's baby momma, laying claim to the guy's paycheck for the next eighteen years. In his time with the Corps, he'd seen more good men make bad decisions than he cared to think about. He prided himself on not being one of them. He wouldn't rule out a chance encounter with a hot guy though. Someone to dream of in the desert. Someone to replace the fantasies he harbored in regard to a certain corporal who had recently been assigned to his unit.

When it came to David Turner, Rick's thoughts didn't border on inappropriate. They 100 percent crossed the line into enemy territory—without backup. Not that he'd ever, in a million years, do anything about the attraction. The last thing he wanted was anyone in the unit to feel uncomfortable around him, so he'd keep his crazy fantasies to himself. And he'd stay the fuck as far away from Cpl Turner as circumstances allowed.

Rick took a seat at the bar and ordered a beer. It had been so fucking long since he'd had one, he held the bottle, savoring the cold weight of it before lifting it to his lips. The first long draw sent his taste buds into orgasm, so he did it again, draining the bottle. He signaled for another. This time, he let the flavor linger before swallowing. The process brought to mind one of his favorite fantasies—him, on his knees, taking a slow taste of a certain Marine's cock.

Fuck. This wasn't working. The whole reason for coming to this particular bar had been to find some eye candy. Cultivate some new fantasies to override the ones he, in no way, could take with him to Iraq.

Rick twisted his stool around, checked out the mass of bodies packing every inch of the space allotted. The place had really filled up since he'd arrived. Music, courtesy of a DJ atop a raised platform in the back, pounded through the speakers, inviting patrons to dance. Quite a few had succumbed to the offer, making the dance floor into a writhing pit of indecency. Rick sipped his beer, admiring a cute ass here and there when one swung toward him. The place attracted an eclectic group, which was fine by him. His daily world thrived on conformity in everything. It was nice to be surrounded by guys in civilian clothes and with actual hair on their heads. Thank fuck, he didn't see a military high-and-tight haircut anywhere until he swung back around and caught a glimpse of himself in the mirrored barback.

Yeah, that right there probably accounted for the empty stools on either side of him. Nothing screamed military like a Marine haircut. Among the gay community, military types often received a cold shoulder. He couldn't blame them. Historically, the armed forces hadn't welcomed alternative lifestyles with open arms, and despite advances in that area, most gay service members preferred to remain in the closet with the door firmly shut. Rick congratulated himself on at least cracking the door every once in a while, to take a peek at the outside world. Like tonight.

He'd have a few more beers. Maybe find someone to dance with. Haircut aside, guys rarely refused a little no-strings grope and grind. And if things went well, perhaps he'd spend a few hours creating some memories to take to the desert.

He was working on his third beer when someone claimed the stool next to him. Rick lifted his gaze to the mirror and damn near choked on his drink.

Shit. Fuck. God-blessed-damn.

What was *he* doing there?

Rick ducked his head, knowing full well it was way too late to yell *incoming!* The fucking bomb had already landed. All that was left to do was pray and prepare to be blown to bits.

Corporal David Turner signaled the bartender, inquired about the quality of the local brews then proceeded to down one—all without acknowledging Rick's presence. Like it was a coincidence he'd sat next to the only other Marine in the bar. But it had to be a coincidence, didn't it? No way was the man gay.

Rick had been trained to assess situations quickly—to calculate the odds and make decisions based on his best judgement. It was a good thing his enemy wasn't armed because Rick would be a dead man. Hell, maybe the bomb had already exploded. Didn't the experts say you'd never know? One minute you were breathing and cracking jokes with your buddies, and the next you were standing in line at the pearly gates? Rick closed his eyes and prayed that to be the case. Death had to be better than spending the next year in close quarters with a man who knew his deepest, darkest secret—a man Rick couldn't stop fantasizing about.

Rick finished his beer then dug a twenty out of his pocket to cover his tab. Just as he placed his hands on the polished wood to push himself away from the bar, the man beside him clamped a paw around Rick's wrist hard enough to spike his temper. Rick jerked his arm, and Dave let him go. He was about to give the corporal shit when the man slid off his stool, crooked his head toward a hallway marked bathrooms, and started walking.

The darkened hallway swallowed the man whole while Rick remained glued to the barstool. He'd been in enough life-or-death situations to recognize the adrenaline rush brought on by fear. Some guys lived for the rush; Rick wasn't one of them. He welcomed the extra energy and the heightened awareness that had saved his ass more than once, but in this instance, the urge to flee, to get the hell out of here while he still could, almost overwhelmed him.

Shit, the man looked fucking fuckable in civilian clothes. The starched button-down dress shirt stretched across broad shoulders and did nothing to hide the hard body beneath. Hard because that was the only option in the Corps. Tight jeans with a dark wash molded to a backside meant to be fucked. Goddamn, the strength evident in his swagger was a turn-on. Rick resisted the urge to massage the massive erection he'd sported ever since the lethal bomb named David Turner sat down beside him.

Fuck me.

Rick stood.

He'd had more confidence storming buildings in search of terrorists than he had following his fellow Marine in a crowded bar. He went into combat with his armor and a small arsenal strapped to his body—and he never went in alone. Wearing only jeans and a stupid fucking BlackWing concert T-shirt, he'd never been more vulnerable. Yet his feet still propelled him toward the unknown. Was he in for an ass-kicking, or did Turner have something else in mind?

Whatever it was, he would find out soon enough.

At the end of the dimly lit hallway, Corporal Turner held a door open for him. Rick brushed past him into the alley only to have his face shoved against a brick wall. Turner breathed in his ear. "Don't say a fuckin' word, Lance Corporal Ingram, you fuckin' cock tease. Do not turn around. Do not fuckin' look at me. Do exactly as I say, and no one will ever know your secret. Nod if you hear me."

Rick nodded.

"Pants down, Marine. Spread 'em and fuckin' show me your hole."

Rick's hands shook like he'd been too fucking close to an incoming mortar round, but he managed to unbuckle his belt and shove his jeans and boxers to his knees. Then, like a good Marine, he followed orders. Bent at the waist, he used one hand to brace against the wall and the other to expose himself.

Turner hocked up a loogy and spit it out. The wad of saliva hit the bullseye and slid along Rick's crack, sending a shudder of desire up his spine to his nape. From there, it ricocheted straight to his already hard as fuck dick. A single digit worked the lubricant past the tight muscles. "Fuck. Goddamnit, Lance Corporal, your ass is fine."

Trembling like a fucking virgin, Rick swallowed a curse and scrunched his eyes shut, envisioning the scene. He hoped to god there weren't any cameras nearby, but who the fuck was he kidding? He'd give anything to see David Turner's cock. To see the look on his face when he came. To witness the man's surrender to his basest desires. God, that would be hot as fuck.

Rick gasped as a second finger joined the first, scissoring to stretch him.

Do it. Fuck the preliminaries. Breech the goddamn door!

He no longer cared about the consequences. Fuck the Marines. Fuck the whole Corps. His cock throbbed. Need held his balls in a vise.

"Gonna tap it, Marine. Gonna tap it hard."

In the distant recesses of his mind, Rick registered the sound of a wrapper ripping, the rattle of a belt buckle, and the rasp of a zipper. Fabric sliding against flesh. Then big, hot, callused hands gripped his ass cheeks—forced them wide.

"Brace yourself. Easy ain't in my vocabulary."

More than ready to be fucked, Rick flattened both palms on the brick wall. The rough baked clay scraped his palms, but he couldn't have cared less as Turner's cock pressed against his tight entrance. A moment of pressure then he tunneled in like a goddamn bunker buster. Fast. Hard. A huge motherfucker meant to destroy on impact.

He might have blacked out. Pain. So much goddamn pain. Followed by pleasure. White. Hot. A fucking heat-seeking missile streaking from his balls through his cock. He came hard, embarrassingly fast, shooting his wad onto his shirt, the fucking wall, every goddamn place imaginable. So much cum he'd need a goddamn IV to replace the lost fluids. Yet Turner kept on. Driving into him like a battering ram. Cursing every time he bottomed out, his bull balls slapping against Rick's shriveled ones.

Turner dug his fingers into Rick's hips hard enough to bruise. His thrusts became erratic. Rick's entire being focused on the pole up his ass. The fucking amazing pleasure/pain. The eroticism of the moment. He'd give anything to see Turner's face. To see what he did to the man. A primal cry burst from the big man's chest. He hammered in again. A string of curses filled the dank air in the alley as Turner emptied himself into the condom.

Still impaled, Rick fought the urge to cry. Because it happened or because it was over? Both? He didn't know, but Marines didn't fuckin' cry. Even when they'd been fucked to within an inch of their life. His fuckin' hole would never be the same, yet he couldn't help thinking that was a good thing.

Hands gripping his hips eased. Slid beneath his shirt to soothe his back muscles then down to caress the crest of his ass. Heartbreakingly tender after such a brutal assault.

"Best goddamn fuck, ever." The breathless words penetrated Rick's post-orgasmic haze, sent a shiver along his spine. Turner retreated, leaving a gaping hole to mark where he'd been.

Rick kept his face to the wall, listened as the corporal righted his clothes. Waited for more orders.

A slap to his ass. "You all packed, Marine?"
Rick nodded.

"No, you're fuckin' not. Lube and condoms. Lots of them. I'm not finished with your ass." Cpl. Turner exited the alley, leaving Rick there to assess the damage.

CHAPTER ONE

Rick exited the church behind the bride and groom with Melody Travis on his arm. "I'm glad that's over," he confessed as they cleared the last pew. He wouldn't have put on a monkey suit and stood in front of a packed church for anyone other than Jake or Will. His older brothers were all the family he had, and he'd do anything for them.

Mel's laughter rang out in the vestibule. "Poor thing. Was it that bad?"

Hell, yes. "I've been through worse." No lie there. At least no one had shot at him, and nothing had blown up. Yet.

They hurried out the front door. Limos waited at the curb to carry the guests to the reception being held in a giant tent out at Melody and Hank's place. The wedding party made an abrupt turn at the foot of the steps, making their way around the corner of the building where they would reenter through a side door to take pictures in the empty church.

Melody tightened her grip on his arm. "Thank you for your service."

Rick nodded, uneasy accepting gratitude for his stint in the Marines. He was proud of the years he'd served his country, would always be a Marine at heart, but those days were behind him. He'd fulfilled a dream and come back a different man. Older. Wiser. Changed in fundamental ways he didn't discuss with anyone. The Marine Corps had taken a green recruit and forced him into their mold, and in doing so, compelled him to grow up, to accept things about himself no amount of discipline or routine could alter.

"Jake said you were in the Marines?"

"Yes, ma'am."

"I bet you turned heads in your uniform."

If you only knew. He held the door for her then followed her inside the small office space off the sanctuary. "I wouldn't know, ma'am."

The woman whirled on him, the skirt of her blue bridesmaid's dress caressing his calf before settling. She fingered the lapel of his tux. "He's modest, too."

The mischief in her smile set him on edge. He knew what was coming next and was powerless to stop it. Why did every married woman think it was their god-given duty to fix up every single man?

"Have you met Sunny's cousin, Amanda? She's about your age and single." She adjusted his boutonniere. "I'll introduce you at the reception. She's got the same blonde hair as Sunny. God," she gushed, "you two will look splendid together."

He would have told her she needn't bother with an introduction since Sunny had thrown her cousin at him the minute the girl arrived in town, but was saved from replying when the bride's parents entered behind them. Apparently, that was the signal the photographer had been waiting for. He ushered everyone into the sanctuary. Rick stood where he was told. Smiled on command. If the Marines had taught him anything, it was that a well-planned mission was a successful one, so he spent every interminable second of the photo shoot planning his next mission—Operation Avoid Matchmaker Melody. He'd prefer to skip the reception altogether, but Jake would murder him, so the best plan he could come up with relied on avoiding Melody Travis as much as possible.

Just because he hadn't brought a date to Jake's wedding didn't mean he needed help getting one. He'd never been short on companionship, but he wasn't going to stand by and let some busybody fix him up at a wedding reception. Even if this Amanda person were interested, nothing could come of them meeting. Looking for the one person he had no business seeking out, Rick swept his gaze over the round tables set with silver, crystal, and fancy china, settling on a table in the back. The stray singles, he surmised. Made sense they'd all be seated together. Avoid-at-all-cost Amanda was one of them, along with a couple of Jake's lawyer friends, including the one his brother had recently hired to take on his workload.

Rick allowed his gaze to linger on the man. A few years younger than Rick, the junior lawyer looked fine in a dark three-piece suit that set off his pale skin and blond hair styled to within an inch of its life—probably with some fancy product with a French name. His trendy glasses screamed designer label.

The only designer duds Rick had ever worn had been provided by Uncle Sam and came in two color-distinctive patterns—woodland and desert. These days he preferred discount store T-shirts, sturdy denim jeans, and steel-toed boots. Stan, Willowbrook's only barber, cut his hair but only when needed—like for a wedding. Jake had threatened to kick his ass if he didn't get a haircut in time for the wedding. Poor Brent was in for a rude awakening. Willowbrook wasn't his kind of town.

One of the Houston lawyers held everyone's attention at the table then, as if on cue, they all burst out laughing. Brent turned toward the infamous Amanda, said something to her, then the two of them weaved their way through the tables to the dance floor. From the looks of things, those two would keep each other occupied for the remainder of the evening. Just as well. Rick didn't hit on heterosexuals. Hell, he didn't hit on anyone. Never had. His one relationship had developed all on its own. A real magnets-and-steel cliché. As the couple danced to a sappy ballad, Rick drained the last of his champagne and silently congratulated himself on a narrow escape. He stuck it out to the end, but as soon as the lights of the limo carrying the newlyweds to the airport disappeared, he loosened his bow tie and made for the car his brother had left for him the night before. It saved Rick hunting up a ride home, and he'd need it to pick up the honeymooners when they returned in a couple of weeks. Even if there had been room in the old pickup Rick used for work, Jake refused to ride in it.

Having said goodbye to those who mattered, he didn't think twice about skirting the crowded tent. He'd successfully avoided Melody's matchmaking, so now it was time to get the hell out of here. If his luck held, he'd make it to Dallas in time to share a couple of drinks with his buddy from the Marines. David's new job, working for a firm that installed security systems for businesses, often brought him to the area. Rick's body hummed with excitement at the opportunity to spend time with Dave. They'd met six years ago when Dave had been assigned to Rick's unit. Prior to their first deployment together, things had turned personal between them—a secret they kept over multiple deployments. Rick had separated from the military first, having had enough of risking his life in the desert. Dave had followed almost a year later when his contract ran out. Rick would be lying if he said he didn't hold out hope of something more than the occasional hookup when Dave's job brought him to Dallas, but neither of them was ready to open the closet door.

Rick stopped at home long enough to change into his best jeans, the ones with a dark wash, and a long-sleeved Henley. Anticipating spending the night, he shoved a clean pair of underwear and his toiletry kit into a backpack. At the last minute, he chucked a box of condoms in on top then he texted his longtime lover to let him know he was on the way. He smiled when Dave responded with his hotel and room number. His luck was definitely holding. No clubbing tonight. A few drinks from the minibar then a night of private debauchery suited him just fine. Tomorrow was Sunday, and with Jake on his honeymoon and Will cozying up with MacKenzie, no one would be expecting to see his face until Monday morning. Life was good.

Until it wasn't.

The instant Dave opened the door, Rick knew something was wrong. He stepped inside, dropped his backpack, and wrapped his arms around Dave's waist, dragging his hard body tight against him. When Dave didn't return the hug, Rick's heart dropped to his toes. He stepped back, taking in the red eyes, the deep lines etched into the beloved face. "What's wrong? Did someone die?"

Dave shook his head. His lower lip trembled, and damn if that didn't shoot a lightning bolt of fear down Rick's spine. "Are you sick?" He cradled his lover's face in his palms. "I'm imagining all kinds of scary shit here, babe. Tell me."

"I can't."

In all the years he'd known David, he'd never heard him utter those words. There wasn't *anything* Staff Sergeant Turner couldn't or wouldn't do. If you looked up the word badass in the dictionary, you'd find a picture of Dave. No mission was too dangerous or impossible. Rick still had nightmares about the shit his best friend and lover had done with him at his side. That they were both alive and still had all their body parts was nothing short of a miracle Rick thanked the universe for every day.

Rick grasped the broadest shoulders he'd ever seen then let his hands fall to lace his fingers with his lover's. "Come." He tugged the big man from the alcove to bed. "Sit the fuck down and tell me what's going on." He was going for tender, but his words came out sounding more like an order. Whatever.

The former Marine dropped to the mattress. He leaned forward, braced his elbows on his knees, and cradled his head in his upturned hands. Rick dragged the desk chair over and sat. Offering support, he wrapped his fingers around the other man's wrists and squeezed.

Dave wasn't a cologne sort of guy, the lack of artifice making his natural musk all the more potent. Despite the fear clawing at Rick's innards, his dick responded to the earthiness of the man. "There isn't anything we can't face together, babe. So, spit it out."

Dave shook his head, and his back heaved as great, gulping sobs ravaged his body.

"Did you kill somebody? What the fuck, man? Talk to me."

"No. No. No."

Rick sat back, observing the broken man before him. "No, you didn't kill somebody, or no, you won't tell me?"

"Both." The usually verbose man couldn't seem to come up with a full sentence.

Gentle wasn't working. Time to try a different tactic. "Fuck you, Staff Sergeant." Rick lunged, catching the larger man off guard, and flattened him on the bed. Climbing astride, one of their favorite positions, he pinned Dave's wrists to the mattress. He leaned over, getting right in his face. "We're a team, fuckwad. Tell me what the fuck is going on. Do I need to kick somebody's ass? What?" Yeah, there was nothing tender about that. The hard ridge of the man's cock lined up with his own burgeoning erection. Whatever was going on, it hadn't affected Dave's libido. Nothing ever had.

Rick shifted gears again, pressing soft kisses to tear-ravaged cheeks. "It's okay, babe. I'm here. You can tell me."

The tender words only made the man blubber harder.

What. The. Ever-loving. Fuck?

Rick trailed kisses along the strong jaw, down the corded neck then back up to the sensitive spot behind his ear—the one that never failed to get Dave's motor running full throttle. "Babe," he whispered then flicked his tongue out to tickle that one special spot.

That was all it took. The beast beneath him growled, reared up, and tossed Rick over onto the bed, pinning him in a grip he had no chance of overcoming. The man may have been a civilian now, but he kept in shape. His muscles had muscles—one of the things Rick admired most about the body pressing him into the comforter.

No words were spoken. None were needed. Sex was a language they both spoke fluently. Dave straddled him. His hot breath fanning Rick's face. His red eyes searching, not for permission, that was a given, but for something else Rick couldn't name. Didn't want to name because his gut told him it would shatter him just as it had shattered the man he loved.

.

CHAPTER TWO

Clothes vanished like the sex fairy had waved a magic wand. Dave positioned Rick where he wanted him, on his back, his knees wide and at his shoulders, then he shoved his dick up Rick's ass like a battering ram to a fortified door. No condom. No lube. No preliminaries. Rick refused to wince at the pain in his ass or his heart. This was too much like their first time. The night before their first deployment together, Dave had taken out months of frustration on Rick's ass in the alley behind a bar. The encounter had left Rick shaken, embarrassed, and after the shock wore off, determined to get to know the then corporal better.

Over multiple deployments, the two became inseparable. Best friends, teammates, secret lovers. They'd seen shit. Done shit. And fucked each other's brains out. They talked about their families, their hometowns, growing up, any and everything save one. Dave Turner didn't talk about his feelings. He fucked them out. Rick had been the recipient of every fuck Dave could give.

The *fuck that was good* fuck.
The *fuck I'm the best motherfucker on the planet* fuck.
The *fuck that image out of my brain* fuck.
The *fuck you* fuck.
The *fuck the Marines* fuck.
The *fuck the desert* fuck.
The *fuck I miss my family* fuck.
The *fuck I hate you* fuck.
The *fuck I need you* fuck.
The *fuck I love you* fuck.
The *fuck I hate myself* fuck.

The list was endless. As his lover powered into him with mindless brutality, Rick called upon everything he knew about the man and came to one conclusion. If their first fuck had been a *fuck you're mine* fuck, then this one had to be a *fuck I don't want to let you go* fuck.

But he *would* let Rick go. The tears were the key. David Turner didn't cry. Whatever had brought Dave to this point, it was eating him up inside, yet the decision had been made. Once committed to a mission plan, David didn't change his mind.

Tamping down the need to scream, the need to rage against an outcome he had no say in, Rick stroked his aching dick and stared into his lover's eyes. The pain harbored there only served to harden Rick against the inevitable. No way in hell was he letting the bastard off easy. Holding his gaze captive, Rick let him see the suffering already brewing deep in his gut. He let him see his heart shattering into a million pieces. He let him see the gaping wound opening in his chest. He let him see the disappointment.

I loved you, asshole.
I gave you everything.

And this is how you repay me.

A goodbye fuck in a hotel room.

Fuck you.

When Dave succumbed and released his self-loathing in hot spurts, Rick came, fiery ribbons of emotion directed at his lover's chest and abdomen. Marking him one final time.

Dave wiped tears from his cheeks, glanced at the streaks of white jizz on his torso. With a silent nod of acceptance, he withdrew and flopped to his back beside Rick.

The scent of sex and their mingled sweat hung heavy in the atmosphere. Heart racing, Rick focused on his survival training. *Breathe. In. Out. Remain still. Breathe. In. Out. Wait. Wait. Wait until the enemy makes the first move. Breathe. In. Out.*

Beside him, the enemy lay still, his arms folded to shield his eyes from whatever harsh reality he was trying to come to terms with. Rick waited, his heart breaking more with each passing minute, until Dave delivered the kill shot.

"I'm engaged. To the girl from my parents' church."

CHAPTER THREE

Rick stumbled into the bar, not entirely sure how he'd gotten there. Everything between David's confession and this moment was a blur. He vaguely recalled getting dressed while Dave cried and pleaded with him to understand. The pressure was too much. It was easier to give in than to stand up for himself. For *them*. It would be alright. They could continue to meet like they had been. She wouldn't change anything. There'd been more, but he'd successfully tuned most of it out, but his parting shot rang like an air-raid siren in his ears. "Don't act like the scorned lover, Rick. It's not like you were going to come out of the closet for me."

The concussive force of that direct hit followed Rick out of the room, to the elevator, and out to the street where he'd somehow summoned an Uber. He'd given the address of the first place that came to mind.

Nothing said *leave me the fuck alone* like claiming the stool situated next to the wall on the end of the bar. The barkeep wandered over. Rick ordered two fingers of Jack Black, downed the whole thing with one swallow then signaled for a refill while the whiskey seared the lining of his esophagus.

"Bad day?" the affable bartender asked as he poured the refill.

"Don't want to talk about it."

"Don't have to. Just letting you know I'll cut you off when you've had enough. You drive yourself here?"

He shook his head. At least he'd had the foresight to leave Jake's car in the hotel parking garage.

The barkeep slid a piece of paper and a pen across the polished wood. "Write down where you want to go when you leave here. I'll hand it to the cab driver when the time comes."

Rick nodded. "Okay. Okay. Sounds good." He scribbled the name of a hotel chain, pushed the paper away. "Closest one will do." He dug out his credit card, handed it over. "Just stick it in my pocket when you cart me out of here."

The credit card and slip of paper disappeared into the register drawer. He hoped the guy would add a generous tip for himself. Then he shot back half of drink number two.

He might have been on his third or fourth and no closer to obliterating the night's events from his memory when his friendly keeper plopped a hamburger and fries in front of him. He didn't ask questions, just ate it, washing the food down with the Daniels family's finest. He should have chosen a different bar. Memories of evenings spent here with Dave crept out of hiding to torment his already tortured soul.

He poured liquor on the flames of his life—to no avail. There wasn't enough liquor in Texas to drown out Dave's last words.

Rick had known about the girl. Dave's ultra-religious parents had been nagging him for years to leave the Corps. They'd encouraged the girl to write to him. Sappy letters the two of them laughed about. As religious as his folks, she was saving herself for her husband—on her wedding night. God, they'd laughed themselves silly over that one. She had no idea the kind of man she was writing to. Debauched Dave. He sucked cock like a Hoover and fucked ass like a demon. Under the right circumstances, he begged Rick to fuck him hard enough to make him forget whatever deviled him at the time. Dave couldn't see himself tied down, and he damn sure wasn't going to marry some skirt-wearing, Bible-thumping, woman.

His parents didn't know, and he wasn't going to tell them. On the few occasions he went home, he'd played the happy bachelor and kept the closet door locked tight.

Rick couldn't imagine what kind of pressure had compelled Dave to propose. It had to be some deep shit to make a guy like him denounce everything he was and veer down a road lined with misery and discontent. Unwilling to admit his own refusal to open the closet door in any way justified Dave's actions, and Rick raised his glass in a mock toast. "Fuck you, Dave." As he downed the last drops in his glass, a familiar silhouette across the room caught his attention.

He squinted to get a better look. Blond hair. Glasses. Fancy duds. *Sin-in-a-suit.* Where did that thought come from, and where had he seen the man before? If his present was looking fuzzy around the edges, his past, at least the immediate past, thankfully, was shrouded in dense fog. Fuck! Why couldn't he remember? If he hadn't been plastered, he'd go over, ask the guy to dance. Maybe end the night in the back alley. A new beginning.

Vague images of the man dancing—with a woman— peeked through the alcohol haze. A name popped into his head. Cousin Amanda. Yeah. Sin-in-a-suit had danced with Amanda.

Where?

"Last one." The barkeep's baritone broke through the haze. Rick shook his head, jerking his much-used tumbler out of reach before the man could provide another refill. Time to cut himself off. Somewhere amid the pain lurked something important. He clenched his jaw tight. Resting his elbows on the bar, he linked his fingers and used his thumbs like a vise on his temples.

Think. Think. Think.

"You okay?"

"Coffee. Water. Something." Rick barked the order, waving the bartender away. Something deep in his gut, besides the fine whiskey he'd consumed, told him the lost memory was important. The rich scent of coffee wafted beneath his nose. He grabbed the cup like a drowning man grasping for a lifeline and sipped. Once. Twice. Again. When he chanced a glance at the man, he'd turned, and their gazes locked. As he peered into the most intense green eyes he'd ever seen, the elusive memory surged out of the blasted haze in all its gut-clenching Technicolor glory. Jake's wedding. A sea of people. Crystal. Silver. Flowers every fucking where. Matchmaking Melody. Cousin Amanda to be avoided at all costs dancing with *him*. Brent something or other. The junior attorney Jake hired to take over most of his brother's accounts.

Rick froze like a deer in the headlights. Blinded.

Oh fuck.

He vaulted off the stool, threading his way through tables and chairs that fucking wavered on a floor that bucked and shifted beneath him. Patrons cursed his stumbling gait, shoved at him.

Fuck. Fuck. Fuck.

He had to get to him. Explain.

He stood face-to-face with Sin-in-a-suit. Up close, he was even sexier than he'd been from a distance. Drunk or not, his body responded in the most primal way possible. Impossible, his brain argued. He loved David. Impossible, beyond his reach, David. The fucking asshole who'd dumped him for a life he couldn't live. Fuck him.

Rick teetered. Sin-in-a-suit reached out, splayed his hands on his chest. "Whoa. Steady." A sympathetic smile graced the younger man's lips and his green eyes behind stylish glasses sparkled with mischief…and recognition. "Hey, you're Jake's brother. Right? William?"

"Richard. Rick," he corrected.

"That's right. Hey, fancy meeting you here. Nice wedding."

Rick leaned in. Last thing he needed was everyone hearing their conversation. "We need to talk," he whispered. At least, he thought it was a whisper. Maybe not.

The guy standing way too close to Sin glanced at Rick then back to Sin. "I'll let you two catch up. Save me a dance?"

Sin nodded. "Later." He turned his less-than-joyful countenance on Rick. "This better be good. I was going to get laid. Like, sure thing. If you screwed that up, you're going to have to make it up to me."

Fuck. Was he implying what Rick thought he was? God, he wished he'd limited himself to two drinks. Nothing like going into battle fucked up. God, he was fucked up. He didn't know which one of them was swaying. He grabbed at Sin, clamped a hand around his bicep. Best to get this over with as soon as possible. He tried for another whisper. "You can't tell anyone."

Those sinful green eyes narrowed. "Tell anyone what?"

Confused, Rick spelled it out. "That you saw me here. Dude. You gotta keep your mouth shut."

A shit-ton of emotions paraded across Sin's face. Understanding. Pity. Regret. Maybe Rick imagined that last one. What did Sin have to regret? Rick had enough regrets to fill a fucking dump truck. "You curious, or is this your thing?"

"Curious?" What the hell was he talking about? "Fuck, no."

Sin nodded. "Then your secret is safe with me." He made a show of zipping his lips shut and throwing away the key. "Richard Ingram was not shit-faced in a gay bar a few hours after his brother's wedding."

"That's right." Rick smiled so hard his face hurt. "Thanks, man. Your secret is safe with me, too." The room spun. He stumbled, would have smashed into a table full of people if Sin hadn't caught him in time.

"How much did you have to drink?"

"Not enough." He clamped a hand to the top of his head to keep it from exploding. "Not nearly enough if I can still feel this shitty."

"Fuck. This is not how I wanted this night to end." He shoved Rick backward and into a chair. "Sit the fuck down. You got a tab at the bar?"

"Yeah. Why? You want a drink?"

"No, I don't want a drink." He blew out a breath. "Stay here. Don't move an inch. I'll be right back."

CHAPTER FOUR

Brent drew the bartender's attention. "You got a tab for Richard Ingram? Says he gave you his credit card."

"Yeah. I got it. Why?"

"He's had enough." He gestured to the corner table where Rick slumped, his forehead resting on crossed arms. "I'm taking him home. Can you close it out?"

"You a friend of his?"

"Sort of. Don't worry. I'll take care of him."

"What's your name?"

"Brent Whitehall. I'm an attorney. I'm in the process of moving here from Houston. I'll be working with his brother Jake over in Willowbrook as soon as I get settled. We were both at Jake's wedding a few hours ago. Don't know why Rick is here and skunk drunk, but I'll see he gets home safe."

"You got some ID?"

What was with this guy? He'd never envisioned handing the first of his new business cards to a nosy, overprotective bartender, but he slid the fancy embossed rectangle across the polished wood anyway. "You his keeper or something?"

"Nah. Just looking out for him. Do it for all my regulars."

Brent hoped his lawyer face hid his surprise at the unexpected bit of news. He'd assumed Rick to be homo-curious or maybe bi. Being a regular at one of Dallas's well-known gay bars suggested something else entirely. "Does he always come in alone?"

"Nah. Usually meets some big guy. Ex-military type. Bookends. A matching pair, those two."

Another piece of the puzzle. Brent added a generous tip to the total then signed the charge slip. "He got stood up tonight?"

The bartender took the signed ticket, slid it into a slot beneath the register. "Don't know. Figured something was going on. He was hell-bent on getting plastered from the get-go. I asked if he drove himself here, and he said he hadn't, so I had him write down where he wanted to go when he left. Told him I'd pour him into a cab. Looks like you're going to save me the trouble." He slapped two pieces of paper on the bar then pointed to the stool Rick recently vacated. "Don't forget his jacket."

Brent picked up the bar receipt and the accompanying scrap of paper containing the name of a popular mid-priced hotel chain sans specific location. "Thank you. You're a good man…"

"Benjamin. This is my place. I take care of my boys."

Brent smiled and tapped the bar. "Nice to meet you, Benjamin. If you need any legal services, give me a call. I'll do right by you." He grabbed Rick's coat then threaded his way through the maze of tables to where the youngest of the

Ingram brothers dozed. He shook him awake. "On your feet, soldier. It's time to go."

Rick raised his head. "Marine. Noz a fuc-fuckin' solzier."

He mentally snapped another piece of the Rick Ingram puzzle into place. "Whatever. Can you stand?"

"Fuck, yez."

He did, but it wasn't pretty. Brent wrestled him into his coat then shrugged on his own. He wrapped an arm around his waist to steady him then Rick slung an arm over Brent's shoulder, and the two of them stumbled into the night. Brent had parked his car down the block. If he could get the idiot there, he stood a decent chance of dropping him off somewhere and still having enough time to return to the bar and pick up where he'd left off.

Getting the drunk into the passenger seat of his Corvette took longer than he'd anticipated. He kept trying to go in headfirst, and no amount of reasoning could convince him it was a bad idea. Giving up, Brent let him do it his way, failing to rein in his amusement as the man squirmed and twisted his large frame until he settled into the seat, exhausted from his efforts.

Brent settled into the driver's seat. He buckled his passenger in first then secured his own seat belt. "You have a hotel room? Some place you can sleep this off?"

Rick gave an exaggerated head shake. "Nah. Dis izgood." He dropped his head against the headrest and closed his eyes.

Brent elbowed him. "You are not sleeping in my car."

He cranked the engine, turned up the heat then got out his phone and looked up the nearest location for the chain hotel Rick had given Benjamin. There was one two blocks over. A phone call ascertained they had a room available.

"You're in luck, buddy," he muttered as he pulled away from the curb. "Gonna get you settled then I'm out."

Brent declined the fancy suite in favor of a standard room without a view. If they'd had a bed in a broom closet, he would have taken that. Rick wasn't going to know one way or the other. All he needed was a safe place to sleep it off. He handed over Rick's credit card then returned to the parking garage to collect his charge. He'd gone to sleep in the few minutes it had taken to secure a room.

When nothing he did rousted the inebriated man, Brent grabbed a half-empty water bottle from the console and splashed it in the man's face. "Wake the fuck up. It's time to go to bed."

"Fuck!" Rick came up swinging. His wrist connected with the car frame with a sickening thud.

"Serves you right." Brent grabbed him by the neck of his shirt and yanked him out of the vehicle. Rick stumbled but righted himself with the aid of the car door.

"Whatz dis?" he asked as they drunk walked to the elevator that would take them to the lobby level.

"Hotel." Brent leaned his charge against the back wall of the paneled car then punched the "L" button.

He wagged a pointer finger in Brent's face. "Nasleeingwizyoudude."

Brent rolled his eyes. "Wouldn't sleep with you if you were the last drunk on the planet."

They reached the lobby and successfully switched elevators to the upper floors.

"Whazwrongwizme?" The insult in his voice would have been comical under different circumstances. The former Marine was so far from Brent's type, he might as well have been a Martian.

Brent dragged him out on the fifth floor, consulted the arrow boards then turned left, hoping Rick would follow. The man weighed a fucking ton, and, from what he could tell, it was all muscle. If the lug collapsed in the hallway, he'd have to spend the night there. No way Brent could pick him up on his own. He located the room number written on the sleeve for the keycard and was grateful when Rick stumbled up next to him and successfully followed him inside.

The door closed behind them.

Brent tossed the keycard on the dresser. "I'm done here." He motioned to the bed. "Get some sleep, buddy."

In a blink, he was up against the wall, breathing in Rick's alcohol-tainted breath and, beneath it, the pure scent of sexy-as-hell male.

"Whazwrongwhifme, pwittyboy?"

His vision clouded. Ugh. How could he have forgotten who this guy was? "Pretty boy?" he ground out. Placing both hands on Rick's chest, he shoved as hard as he could. If he'd been sober, Brent couldn't have moved him an inch, but because he was inebriated, the asshole stumbled, ricocheted off the dresser before he fell, landing flat on his back on the end of the bed. Time to set Rick Ingram straight. "I'll tell you what's wrong with you, Jarhead. All you military types are the same. You're self-centered, egotistical assholes with a god complex. Get over yourself."

"Tellmewhazyouwillythink." His eyes rolled back in his head then he passed out cold.

Brent shook him. No response. He tried again. "Shit." Even if he wasn't his new boss's brother, he couldn't leave him like this. Drunks were known to choke on their own vomit if they slept on their back.

Half an hour later, he collapsed in the desk chair. His shirt had come untucked from his trousers and the sweat stains under his pits looked like he'd run a marathon. Wasn't far from the truth. He'd started by removing Rick's shoes. When he still couldn't wake him enough to get him to assist in his own comfort and safety, he dragged and tugged until he'd maneuvered Rick fully onto the bed. In the process, Rick's coat became twisted, so he'd worked that off. The Henley underneath was just as bad, so he'd removed it as well.

Taking a breather, he glared down at the drunken fool. He'd never seen a more perfect human specimen than the one before him. Acres of tanned skin flowed over a sculpted landscape meant to be explored—slowly, reverently. Strong shoulders gave way to defined pecs sprinkled liberally with dark hair. Below that were the rolling hills of his abs. Another spattering of hair around his navel formed an arrow and disappeared below the waistband of his low-slung jeans.

"Lord, have mercy," he whispered. "That's got to be illegal." If he'd taken his shirt off in the bar, the patrons would have eaten him alive. Some out of desire, others out of jealousy.

Shaking off his ridiculous thoughts, Brent consulted his watch. *Shit.* By now the Adonis he'd planned to fuck the rest of the night away with had probably left with someone else. Brent plucked at his shirt. Nobody in his right mind would find him attractive in his current condition. Wrestling with Rick's dead weight had him sweaty and his shirt wrinkled beyond repair.

He rubbed a hand over his face. He'd envisioned a night of hot, no-strings-attached sex before he drove all the way to Houston tomorrow to supervise the packing of his belongings. Nothing about this trip had gone as planned. He still didn't have a place to live in Willowbrook, which, besides the wedding, had been his primary reason for the visit. He'd planned to spend the two weeks of Jake's vacation settling into his new place and reading over current files in his new office.

So much for plans.

Rick groaned, grabbed at his stomach. Afraid the drunk was about to spew his guts up, Brent hooked a finger in a beltloop and tugged the man over onto his side. He piled all the pillows on the bed behind him to keep him from rolling to his back then placed a wastebasket next to the bed.

Exhausted, Brent sank into the desk chair to keep vigil. He couldn't fuckin' sit up all night long, and he didn't feel right leaving him here alone. The wall of pillows wasn't a match for a guy that size. If he rolled, he'd squish them flat, putting himself in danger.

"Fuck me sideways," he growled. He slid his coat on, grabbed the room key, and stomped out the door to get his suitcase. If he was going to spend the night, he'd at least get a shower and have fresh clothes in the morning.

CHAPTER FIVE

The pounding in his head woke Rick. He rolled over and cursed as he landed on a pile of pillows. *What the fuck?* He tossed the offending bedding then cracked one eye open. Light shown through a gap between the drapes, providing enough illumination for a one-eyed inspection. Hotel room. He wracked his brain, trying to recall checking in and coming up blank.

Mentally searching for a place to start, his brain clicked on a solid memory—Jake's wedding. His sappy-in-love brother going weak in the knees at the sight of his bride. A funny-as-hell moment, but no explanation for his present whereabouts or the entire Marine Corps band marching around in his skull. Had he overindulged at the reception?

Memories flooded his brain. Food, champagne toasts, the private, kickass, BlackWing concert for the newlyweds. Celebrities everywhere—friends and relatives of the bride. A bunch of unfamiliar faces—his brother's friends from law school and the firm he'd worked at in Houston for several years. Rick had left there sober with plans to see Dave.

Shit.

Dave.

The same memories he'd tried to drown in a sea of booze rushed to the forefront. Dave's tear-ravaged face as they fucked. His bullshit confession. His excuse for cutting Rick out of his life. His accusations.

The unthinkable popped into his head. His heart skipped a beat. Had he gone back to Dave's room and begged? *Fuck, no. I. Do. Not. Beg.* He *did,* however, drink to forget.

Yeah. He'd gone to the bar, where he and Dave had spent many hours over the last year, with every intention of getting wasted.

Mission accomplished.

He swallowed the bile rising to his throat and searched his pickled memory banks for anything to explain how he'd ended up here. A vague recollection pierced through the haze—a dude pressed against the wall. Eyes as green as winter wheat. His glasses askew and his full, kissable lips saying…something.

Damn. Had he picked somebody up last night? Were they still here?

Shit!

He sat up, knocking something off the nightstand as he groped for the light switch. He flicked the bedside lamp on then immediately wished he hadn't. The soft glow momentarily blinded him. He slapped a hand over his eyes. His eyes slowly adjusted, and he risked a glance at the other side of the bed.

Empty. *Thank, god.* But slept in. *Jesus, what did I do?*

He scrubbed at his face with both hands, trying to recall anything beyond getting shitfaced at the bar. Nothing. Nada. Zip. Damn, he'd fucked up. Perhaps, literally. Tossing the covers aside, he swung his feet to the floor where they landed atop his discarded clothes. All of them. Ahh, shit! He must have been beyond drunk to not remember taking his clothes off—or doing…whatever he'd done.

Naked, he gingerly made his way to the bathroom. He took a piss, washed his hands, and splashed cold water on his face. A glance in the mirror revealed bloodshot eyes complete with dark baggage, sallow skin, and a hairstyle he couldn't pass off as artfully disheveled. In other words, he looked like hell.

And felt like it, too.

He switched on the water in the shower then looked around for the little wrapped bar of soap. Something in the wastebasket caught his eye.

Fuck. Fuck. Double fuck!

Someone, presumably the guy who had shared his bed, had taken the time to shower before leaving. A closer inspection of the small enclosure revealed the used bar of soap resting on the ledge provided for such things. His gaze landed on a damp towel hanging from a wall hook, partially obscured by the open bathroom door.

What. Did. I. Do?

He'd never been so drunk he couldn't recall sleeping with someone. Never. *Oh, Christ! Condom!*

He grabbed the wastebasket beneath the bathroom counter, dumped it out in the sink. Nothing but the soap wrapper.

Shit.

He scurried into the main room, located the waste and recycle bins underneath the desk. Empty.

Shit. Shit. Double shit.

He checked both nightstands.

Picked his clothes up off the floor.

Crawled on his hands and knees to look under the bed.

Tossed all the bedding to the floor.

Nothing. No used condom. No empty wrapper.

He sat on the mattress, rested his elbows on his knees, and cradled his aching head in his upturned hands. Either he hadn't had sex with the person he'd shared the room with, or he'd had unprotected sex.

Another thought made his blood run cold. He grabbed his jeans, fished around for his wallet and keys, sighing in relief when he found them right where they were supposed to be. And in his wallet—the exact amount of cash he expected to see and the emergency condom he was never without even though he hadn't been with anyone other than Dave in years. Still, the *be prepared* lesson his older brothers had practically beat into him when he reached puberty was one he'd taken to heart.

Christ, why can't I remember?

He needed to get home. Forget last night even happened and hope his actions didn't come back to bite him in the ass.

Freshly showered, he pulled on his jeans then yanked his wrinkled shirt over his head. A whiff of a vaguely familiar scent teased his nostrils. He brought the collar to his nose and sniffed. Not his cologne or aftershave. Not Dave's. He drew the scent in again, let it linger on his consciousness. The same obscure memory he'd experienced earlier flashed through his brain—a dude pressed against the wall, glasses askew, kissable lips set in a sinfully handsome face he couldn't for the life of him assign a name to.

He glanced at the entry alcove. He could feel the ugly, textured wallpaper imprinting his palms as he held the guy captive for the span of a heartbeat. Had he kissed him? Dragged him to bed and had his way with him?

Everything he'd seen pointed in that direction.

He brought his shirt to his nose, inhaling the fading evidence. The scent stirred a hazy memory of want and need. His cock, ever its own master, responded.

This was so far from good, it bordered on disaster.

Not having any clue where he actually was, Rick ordered an Uber to take him to the hotel garage where he'd left Jake's car the night before. Waiting at the valet stand for his ride, he fingered the scrap of paper he'd found on the dresser next to the keycard.

The bold scrawl imparted a simple message that was both reassuring and frightening at the same time.

Rick,

Your secret is safe with me.

Brent

Whoever Brent was, he knew Rick's name. Knew he was in the closet. Agreeing to keep Rick's secret meant he knew someone who might find the information interesting. Which meant, they had friends or acquaintances in common.

At least he had a name to go with the face now.

He gave the driver the name and address of the other hotel then closed his eyes against the bright Texas sun. Who the hell was this Brent person? He couldn't recall knowing anyone by that name. Yet, every time the man's visage popped into his mind, Rick's dick stood at attention like it knew the man.

Rick asked to be dropped off at the garage entrance. He didn't know if Dave was still around and didn't want to know. On the drive home, he tried to reconcile himself to the choice Dave had made. He understood, he really did, but he'd believed the man was stronger than to let himself be railroaded into a loveless, passionless, lie of a marriage. No matter how hard Dave tried to push his guilt off on Rick, he liked to think he'd say the hell with what anyone thought before he'd marry a woman he wasn't attracted to, but he couldn't be sure. If Dave had told his parents the truth and asked Rick to be his life partner, would he have come out of the closet?

Yesterday, he probably would have said yes, but today, he wasn't convinced. He chalked his reasoning up to the fuzzy memory of a face, glasses askew, and an enticing scent growing fainter with every passing minute.

There'd been no formal agreement between him and Dave, but he had left the Marines based on Dave's faithless promises to find a way for the two of them to be together in the civilian world. A few hours after learning fearless Dave was more afraid of what his parents thought of him than dying in a godforsaken desert halfway around the globe, Rick had been lusting after another man. Didn't matter he couldn't remember everything that happened. What he did recall was enough to poke holes in the fabric of what he'd thought was the solid cloth of his life.

He loved Dave. Would most certainly have outed himself in order to be with him, if only his lover for the last six years would have done the same.

Six fucking years of sneaking around. Six fucking years of promises and lies.

Rolling the window down, he let the frigid January air whip through the car. The icy blast helped clear away the last vestiges of his hangover. The fog gradually lifted from his brain, revealing the previous night in unrelenting clarity. As before, memories of the wedding were mostly amusing. Seeing his older brother in a panic, worrying his bride would come to her senses and leave him at the altar. The sappy look on Jake's face when he pledged his love for all eternity. Yeah, that right there was funny shit, and he was damn glad he hadn't erased the memories with alcohol. They were prime teasing material not to be messed with.

Knowing he'd be driving to Dallas following the reception, he'd gone easy on the champagne that flowed freely. He'd danced with the bride, and briefly with the groom—a silly moment between brothers that made him smile recalling it. Jake had hugged him tight on the dance floor, rocking side-to-side while whispering insults laced with sentimental I love you's in his ear. He didn't know if Jake had been drunk on happiness or bubbly. Probably a little of both.

After their brothers' dance, Rick returned to his seat on the raised dais where he could keep an eye on things. They'd done a good job of faking out the paparazzi, but with the number of celebrities on hand, anything was possible. All it would take was one social media post to bring the media down on them. So Rick kept watch.

As the miles sped past, he racked his brain for details. His gaze had touched on everyone in the tent at one point or another as they ate, mingled, danced, and toasted the happy couple. He'd known nearly everyone there either in person or by reputation, save the ones seated at a table far in the back. Jake's single friends from his law school days and some colleagues from the firm he'd worked for in Houston right after receiving his law degree. A few had come in the night before for the bachelor party held in Hank's barn turned recording studio. Others had arrived in time for the wedding, and most of them had stopped by the preacher's office where Jake and his groomsmen awaited the nuptials.

A face blasted to the forefront, shaking Rick to the core. His palms grew damp on the steering wheel as he scanned the road for a place to pull over. He'd left the wide freeways behind a while ago for two-lane roads, some with shoulders, others without. A bank of mailboxes up ahead set far enough off the road to be safe. Rick signaled then pulled to the shoulder, kicking up a cloud of dust and debris as he skidded to a halt. He slammed the transmission in to Park then dropped his forehead to the steering wheel, letting the disturbing memories flow like sewage from a burst pipe.

One face. One name stood out from all the sea of people he'd met at the wedding. *Brent.* The fucking junior lawyer Jake hired to take over most of his caseload so he could concentrate on his new bride and the box of unfinished manuscripts under his bed.

Brent. Hauling his drunk ass out of the bar.

Brent. Pressed against the wall, his glasses askew, his kissable lips inches away. His enticing scent weaving a spell past the alcohol-induced haze to set Rick's libido ablaze.

Brent. Pushing him down on the bed. Undressing him.

Rick sat up, stared unseeing into the distance.

"God almighty. Tell me I didn't fuck Jake's new employee."

He bounced his head off the headrest several times in an attempt to shake more memories loose, but there was nothing there. No answer for the questions making him sick to his stomach. If he'd fucked the man, he had no recollection. He fished the handwritten note from his pocket. Read the condemning words again.

Your secret is safe with me.

He crumpled the paper into a ball then flung it across the car. It bounced off the windshield, coming to rest in the passenger seat like a lethal hitchhiker.

Fuck.

Avoiding Brent shouldn't be too difficult, if he put his mind to it. He rarely saw Jake unless they had something planned. Brent would be working in Jake's downtown office. No reason for Rick to go that way other than to visit The Donut Hole or the diner. It was time to change his eating habits anyway. Despite the physical labor required for his job, he'd gained a few pounds since he'd left the Marines. If he kept eating the way he had been, he'd be big as a barn in a couple of years. Better to nip that shit in the bud now while he still had the discipline to stick to a regime.

He took a few more minutes to calm his racing heart before he pulled onto the road. He'd stop at the grocery store, stock up on the essentials. Lots of lean meats to grill. High protein. Low carbs. Maybe he'd take up running in the evenings or early mornings. Or both. Burn off energy and calories. Keep him from thinking about Brent, obsessing about what he had or hadn't done with the man. And, no matter what, he wouldn't seek him out to ask.

Some things were better left in the vast unknown.

CHAPTER SIX

Brent dropped the nearly empty packing tape dispenser on top of the last box then plopped his tired ass onto a barstool at the counter that separated the tiny kitchen of his Houston apartment from equally tiny living space. The movers were due any minute. Everything he owned, save his work clothes and a few casual outfits, would go into storage until he could find a permanent place in Willowbrook. He'd packed everything himself. Not because he couldn't afford to pay someone to do it, but because he needed the physical exertion to keep his mind off things it had no business thinking about. Like his new boss's baby brother.

Stretching sore muscles, Brent limped to the refrigerator. He stared at the meager contents. He'd dumped everything, except a modest supply of beer and water. The beer practically called his name, but he reached for a water bottle instead. Beer made him maudlin, and the last thing he needed right then was to romanticize his situation.

He was moving, goddamnit. Alone. When he'd landed the job in Willowbrook, he'd pictured himself and Kenneth living the small-town life. They'd buy a house with a white picket fence. During the day, Kenn would have all the peace and quiet he needed to draw his comic book characters, and, on the weekends, Brent would mow the lawn. The two of them would tend the flowerbeds then sit on the wide porch and sip cold beers and talk about their week. Maybe they'd have the herb garden they both wanted. And a dog. He'd always wanted a dog, but the nomadic life he'd led growing up hadn't allowed for pets.

He'd envisioned a picture-perfect life. But when he'd asked Kenn to marry him and make his dreams come true, he'd gotten the shock of his life. With a look of horror contorting his beautiful features, his lover of two years turned him down flat. Not just no, but hell, no.

Brent rubbed his chest where the sharp barb of Kenn's arrow still stung. Kenn had begged him to turn the job down, to stay in Houston, but the damage to their relationship had been done. They wanted different things. Brent wanted roots. A home. A family. He'd thought Kenn wanted the same things, but he'd been wrong. So, Brent had taken the job and had been eager to settle into his solo existence in Willowbrook.

Then Rick Ingram happened.

Every cell in his body had taken notice of the ex-Marine when they'd been briefly introduced prior to Jake's wedding. Rick had hardly paid him any mind. At least, that was what anyone else who'd been there would say, but Brent knew better. He'd caught the guy checking him out, his gaze raking him from head to toe, assessing. He'd wondered at the scrutiny, but then he saw that Rick gave every newcomer the same treatment, as if cataloging details in the event they needed to be repeated back to law enforcement later on. He'd chalked it up to the number of celebrities attending on the bride's behalf.

Jake's father-in-law was a well-known Hollywood and Broadway actor, and his friends had turned out for the wedding. Everyone had been a little on edge about strangers. Photo ID that matched the name on the invitation had to be presented in order to get near the church. They weren't taking any chances on paparazzi crashing the nuptials.

Still, he'd been hyperaware of Rick Ingram throughout the ceremony and reception. The man was a god. Dressed in a tux, he had the look of a barely tamed wild man, except when he looked at Jake. Then he resembled a cheerful teddy bear. For as long as he lived, he'd never forget the way Rick had danced with Jake at the reception. With both their parents gone, the Ingram brothers stuck together, as evidenced by the dance. It had been corny as hell, the brothers laughing at each other, Rick playing the stooge, snuggling up to Jake, resting his head on his shoulder, and nibbling at his brother's ear. It had been both hilarious and tender. And all the while, Brent had been hard as stone, imagining Rick holding him on the dance floor. Nuzzling his neck. Whispering sweet nothings in his ear.

Later in the evening, he'd sensed someone's gaze on him, glancing up in time to see Rick's eyes dart away. The man had been watching him from his place on the dais. Brent told himself it was a passing glance. Rick was just being vigilant. Keeping an eye on all the guests. To cover his mounting interest in the man, he'd asked the bride's cousin to dance.

Amanda was a sweet girl. She had a bit part on a TV sitcom and was auditioning for movie roles while trying to earn her place in Hollywood rather than ride the coattails of her famous uncle. She'd pegged him as gay immediately and latched on to him as protection from the groom's bachelor friends. She had plenty of Hollywood stories to tell and a sweet, bubbly personality that entertained him and kept his eyes and mind from roving to a certain member of the wedding party he had no business fantasizing about. Rick Ingram wasn't gay, which made his thoughts about the man ridiculous *and* inappropriate. He'd left the reception with several needs. He needed a place to spend the night. He needed a drink in the worst way. And, he needed to get laid so he could quit obsessing about his new boss's youngest brother.

He'd put off finding a hotel room, planning to get a drink first and hoping he'd satisfy the need to get laid at the same time. A room might not even be necessary if he hooked up with a local. He'd driven straight to the bar his friends in Houston had assured him was the place to go in Dallas if he was looking for companionship. They'd been right. He'd danced with several prospects and flirted with a few more by the time he'd settled on one Adonis who fit what he was looking for. He was tall, had shoulders broad enough to carry the world, and eyes that hinted at a little mystery hidden behind them. All the while he flirted with the guy, he told himself it was a coincidence he resembled Rick Ingram.

A familiar tingle on the back of his neck had him turning to scan the room . Rick Ingram sat at the bar, staring at him.

Everything had gone downhill from that point on. Rick had drunk stumbled in between Brent and the guy he'd been flirting with. At the time, Brent told himself he was doing a good deed. Making sure his boss's brother didn't spend the night in a gutter, or worse, the drunk tank at the local precinct.

He told himself the lie as he took care of the man's bar tab. As he poured him into his car. As he undressed him and put him to bed. As he lay awake on the other side of the bed, watching him sleep off what had to be an unhealthy amount of alcohol. He stuck to the story as the man rose in the wee hours of the morning, shucked the remainder of his clothes then fell back, oblivious to Brent's presence, into his drunken stupor. He clung to the story as he showered the following morning then slipped from the room, leaving behind nothing but a note meant to reassure.

He'd just passed the last exit for Waco when his carefully crafted story gave way to reality. Rick Ingram was the sexiest man he'd ever laid eyes on. He'd taken care of him that night, not for the altruistic reasons he'd told himself but because he wanted the man. Rick had made it clear he was in the closet with the door firmly closed, which made him completely off-limits. Despite Kenn's defection, Brent hadn't given up hope of finding a partner who wanted the same things he did. The Adonis in the bar had been a short-term distraction. Someone to make him forget, if only for a few hours, the loneliness stretching out ahead of him. Someone to satisfy a physical need. Instead, he'd spent the loneliest night of his life lying next to a man with hairy toe knuckles, lips that begged to be kissed, and the ability to destroy him.

CHAPTER SEVEN

"Fuck! This stuff makes Super Glue look like kids' paste." Rick dropped the dirty plate into the hot, soapy water to soak then grabbed another one from the stack in the other side of the divided sink. He made a mental note to rinse the egg off next time—before it dried to a baked-on finish. Avoiding the downtown area forced him to eat every meal at home, which created lots of dishes. Worth the headache if it kept him from running into Brent whatever his name was.

Thanks to the job he'd done on the house Will's girlfriend rented, his remodeling business had shot through the roof. In the last week, he'd given out countless bids for new work and split his time between two ongoing projects. He'd barely had time to eat, much less clean up after himself. He rinsed the plate in his hand and stuffed it in the already packed dishwasher.

Note to self: Turn the dishwasher on occasionally.

If he'd done that simple task a few days ago, his sink wouldn't be piled high with dirty dishes, and he wouldn't be up to his elbows in suds, trying to salvage what he could.

Another note to self: Buy frozen dinners so I don't have to do this crap.

That would solve the problem.

He fished the soaking plate out and resumed scrubbing. If nothing else, the mindless chore gave him time to think. If his business grew at the rate it was, he'd have to hire help. He didn't know the first thing about being an employer, but like everything in his life, he'd learn.

Where do you go to find experienced help?

That was another thing he'd have to figure out. He didn't have the time to train someone. Whoever he hired had to be able to work independently and be dependable. He wasn't going to fucking babysit a grown-ass adult.

He contemplated the other things that came with being an employer like insurance, workman's comp, and payroll taxes when the front door opened, followed by the slap of the screen door hitting the jamb. His heartrate spiked as adrenaline shot through his system. He dropped the plate into the sink and spun, his wet, soapsuds-coated hands ready to do battle.

"Yo! Rick? You home?"

Shit.

It's only Will.

He turned around, gripped the rim of the sink, and willed his hands to quit shaking.

"Rick?"

"In here." He picked up the plate, placed it into the last available spot in the dishwasher then shoved the rack hard, rattling the dishes. He opened the cabinet door beneath the sink and crouched, scanning the interior for the dishwasher detergent.

"There you are." Will leaned a hip against the counter on the other side of the dishwasher. "Whatcha doing down there?"

"Looking for the dishwasher detergent. Where the hell is it?"

His brother skirted the open appliance door and leaned over his shoulder to grab a plastic bucket. "Right here. Can't you read?"

Rick stood, yanked the container from his brother's hands. "What the fuck is this?"

"Pods." Will pointed to a picture on the front that looked more like a throat lozenge than detergent. "Don't tell me you haven't used the dishwasher since I bought this new stuff."

Pods. What the hell? Ignoring his brother's snide question, Rick tried to pry the lid off the container. Like the dried-on egg, it wouldn't budge. "What the fuck?" He shoved it into Will's midsection. Instinct had his brother reaching for the box. "You bought it. You figure out how to get it open."

Needing a minute to get himself under control, Rick stomped to the refrigerator for a cold soda. He popped the pull tab and guzzled half the can in one long pull. A plastic *pop* from the other side of the room drew his attention. Will had the container open. He pinched a pod between his thumb and forefinger, held it up.

"This is a detergent pod." He placed it in the dispenser then slid the lid closed. "So easy, even a Marine can do it."

"Fuck you." Rick downed the remainder of his soda, crushed the can in his fist then barked out a satisfying belch.

"Who pissed on your Corn Flakes?" Will snapped the lid shut on the detergent and placed it beneath the sink. Using the toe of his boot, he lifted the dishwasher door. When it was high enough to reach without bending over, he gave it a shove to shut it. "Stuck-on shit cycle?"

Rick shrugged.

"I'll take that as a yes." He pushed a couple of buttons. Lights lit up the control panel, and the sound of running water could be heard. Will grabbed a dish towel and wiped the counter before leaning against it. Arms crossed, he eyed his brother in an all-too-familiar stare-down.

Rick didn't have time to wait Will out. He broke within seconds. "Don't you ever knock?"

The brothers had grown up in this house, and though it was Rick's official residence now, Jake and Will thought nothing of walking in uninvited whenever they wanted. He'd lock the door, but they all had keys. *Should have changed the locks when I remodeled the place.* Hindsight was 20/20.

"Why would I do that?" Will's head swiveled as he took in as much of the living space as he could without moving. "Unless you're not alone." He raised an eyebrow in question.

"That's not the point. This is my house now. I'm entitled to a little privacy, don't you think?"

"Nope." Will pushed away from the counter, helped himself to a soda from the fridge.

While he was pouring it down his gullet, Rick asked, "What are you here for anyway? I thought you moved out." Will had been gradually moving in with his girlfriend over the last few weeks. Since all he owned were clothes and a few art supplies, he'd been carrying a box at a time down the block to her house when the mood struck him or he needed something he'd left behind.

"Jake called, wants us both to come down to his office. I figured since I was here, I'd get some more of my stuff."

"What's big brother want?"

Will finished his soda and chucked the empty can at the recycling bin in the corner. It hit the rim then teetered over, landing atop a beer bottle from the sound of it. "Don't know. He said he wanted both of us, so I'm guessing it has something to do with the estate? Can't think of anything else it could be. You?"

He shook his head. "I got nothing."

"Let me grab one of my boxes then let's see what Jake wants so I can get back home to my woman."

Since Will still hadn't purchased a car of his own, he put his box in the bed of Rick's truck. "You going to be okay here alone?"

A sound, part growl, part laugh, came from Rick's lips. "Seriously? I survived the Marines and multiple trips to the sandbox. I don't need a babysitter."

"Didn't think you did, bro. I just feel bad about leaving you on your own. Thought I'd be here for a while longer."

"I know you did. Glad you got your shit together, and glad you found your woman. Kenzie's great." Just because his own life sucked swamp water didn't mean he wasn't happy for Will and Jake. They'd both found their cliché. The woman to complete them. They were happy as pigs in mud, and he was happy for them. Really. He was.

~ ~ ~

There were only two cars in the parking lot in front of Jake's office. Rick steered clear of the cherry-red Corvette and parked next to his brother's boring sedan instead. Even though it was after-hours, the front door was unlocked. The younger Ingram brothers filed inside like they'd done thousands of times before.

The reception desk was empty, though Jean, the legal secretary Jake had inherited along with the business, had left a lamp on. Up until a few months ago, the smaller office closest to the front door had been used as a storage room, but tonight, the door stood open, the faint glow of a desk lamp visible beyond the otherwise dark portal. Rick's heartbeat sped up, and as much as he told himself not to, he still swiveled his head, hoping for a glimpse of his brother's new employee.

Brent sat at his desk, his focus entirely on a document he held, a pencil threaded through the fingers of his right hand. His discarded suit coat hung over the back of his executive chair. He'd loosened his tie and rolled the cuffs of his shirt up to expose his forearms. The glimpse made Rick's mouth dry and his step falter. He'd thought the man attractive even when he'd believed him to be heterosexual. Now that he knew otherwise, he couldn't stop thinking about him, wanting him.

The man was sexy as shit. He'd done Rick a solid the night of Jake's wedding and he'd yet to thank him for getting him out of the bar safely. He'd also like to know what, exactly, he'd done once they left the bar, but he wasn't sure he was ready to hear the details. Maybe one of these days, when Dave's betrayal didn't feel like someone had taken 80 grit sandpaper to his heart. In the meantime, he'd keep his distance from the man.

Rick stepped into his brother's office and, at his nonverbal command, closed the door behind him and took the only unoccupied chair in the room. "You should let me redo this place. It gives me the heebie-jeebies."

It didn't look like Jake had changed a thing since inheriting their father's law practice nearly five years ago. The desk was the same. The ugly carpet was the same. Hell, even the books and knickknacks on the built-in shelves along one wall appeared to be the same.

"Yeah. I should." Jake rubbed a hand over his face bringing Rick's attention to the dark circles under his eyes and the slack muscles around his mouth. "One of these days, I promise. I've got a shit-ton of other stuff to worry about right now."

Will sat forward. "Shit. Did Sunny figure out you're an asshole and leave?"

Jake shot their middle brother a death stare that reminded Rick way too much of their father, who had been an asshole. Jake physically resembled the man, but beneath the outer shell, the two were nothing alike. Thank god. "No, butt face. Everything is fine. Sunny isn't going anywhere."

"Then what's this about?"

The oldest of the brothers rocked back in his chair, his gaze on the ceiling as he blew out a breath fraught with tension. When he brought his weight forward again, he rested his forearms on the desk and laced his fingers together. "I got a call from the D.A. up in New York this afternoon."

In his peripheral vision, he saw Will straighten, his full attention on their brother. "What did he want?"

"He said Jessica made bail."

"How?"

"He didn't know. He was apologetic, said he called as soon as he heard the news. The problem is, this happened nearly two weeks ago. She was supposed to meet with her lawyer earlier this week. When she didn't, and he couldn't locate her, he reported her missing. That's how the D.A. found out she'd been released in the first place."

Will jumped up like a spring from the ancient, upholstered chair had poked him in the ass and stomped over to the plate-glass window behind Jake's desk. At the best of times, the small garden beyond wasn't much to look at. In the dark, he would only see a reflection of himself in the heavy glass.

Rick hated that Will's past wouldn't let him alone. After his fiancée had betrayed him with the help of a gallery owner and, ironically, an employee of Sunny's gallery, he'd come home a mess. Since Rick had been a mess himself, missing Dave, and the Marine Corps, he knew what a mess looked like. The two of them, living in the same house, had been a mopey shitshow until Kenzie had given his brother a reason to live. It broke his fucking heart to see this shit come back on his brother again, after all this time. "What does that mean for Will? And MacKenzie?"

Kenzie's career had been collateral damage in Jessica's scheme to ruin Will. Thanks to Sunny's friendship with Hank and Melody Travis, Kenzie had come to work for Hank in Willowbrook. He wasn't exactly sure how the two had met, but once they did, it was like watching a spark grow into a wildfire.

"It means, we all need to be extra vigilant. There's no reason to believe she'd come here, but we need to be careful, just in case."

"You've told Sunny?" Will spoke, his back still to them and the room.

Jake's wife had been framed by Jessica and her cohorts for the theft of Will's paintings. The private detective Jake hired had found the evidence needed to clear Sunny, and that had ultimately led to the arrest of the culprits and the return of the stolen paintings to Will. "Not yet. I'm going to though. She won't be going anywhere alone until we know where Jessica is. Same goes for MacKenzie."

"I'll see to it," Will said, his shoulders slumping. "I thought this would be over when I burned the paintings. I'm beginning to think it'll never be over. I'm going to have to carry this shit with me the rest of my life."

Jake swiveled his chair to face Will. "She couldn't have gone far. Not without financial assistance. She'll be behind bars again soon."

Will spun around, leaned his shoulders against the glass. "Someone gave her bail money. Who would do that?"

Jake shrugged. "The D.A. said he was looking into that. I'm sure he'll question the person as to her whereabouts."

"I don't like it." Will shook his head. "She's a master manipulator. She must have some other poor soul on the hook, someone she's convinced of her innocence. Where else would she get bail? With a financial backer, she could be anywhere."

"Let's not borrow trouble, Will." Jake stood, clapped a hand on their middle brother's shoulder. "I know this dredges up bad memories, and I wouldn't have told you she'd made bail if they knew where she was. Since they don't, I'd be remiss in not warning you to be vigilant until she's located."

Will nodded. "You're just doing your job, and I appreciate it. I'd never forgive myself if my past mistakes put Kenzie or Sunny in harm's way."

Rick stood and stretched. "We'll keep our eyes peeled for anything out of the ordinary. Maybe we should give the staff at the diner a heads-up. If Jessica comes to town, chances are she'd stop in there or at The Donut Hole. Everybody else does."

"That's a great idea, Rick." Jake scribbled something on a notepad on his desk. "I'll talk to Marge at the diner. You're still friends with Cathy at The Donut Hole, aren't you?"

He'd dated her all through high school. Everyone thought they'd get married. Everyone but him. They hadn't exactly parted on good terms, but since his return to Willowbrook, the owner of the local donut hot spot had been nothing but cordial to him. Still single, maybe she thought she had another chance with him. He'd do anything for his brother, so he answered the only way he could. "Yeah. I'll stop in tomorrow morning and give her a heads-up."

Jake grabbed his suit coat off the back of his chair. "I'll touch base with the local PD tomorrow, too. Give them a heads-up." He shrugged his coat on. "Let's get out of here. I'm tired. It's been a long fucking day."

The three brothers filed out of the office, Jake in the lead, Rick bringing up the rear. As he passed Brent's office, Jake raised his hand in farewell and called out, "Don't stay too late."

"I won't, boss."

The sound of the man's voice sent a shiver of awareness down Rick's spine. *Shit.* Even his deep voice was sexy. Calling it self-preservation, he kept his gaze forward as he passed Brent's office and followed his brothers out into the frigid night.

CHAPTER EIGHT

Shit.

Brent grabbed his jacket and briefcase from the passenger seat, breaking into a run as he neared the courthouse. He was fucking late. Again. Stuck in traffic on the interstate, he'd made the difficult decision to call his boss and ask him to cover for him for the second time in the first month of his employ. The first time he'd been late to a court appearance, there'd been an accident on the freeway and traffic had been at a standstill for hours. He'd had no choice but to alert Jake and have him stand in for him. Today's delay was due to construction on the same stretch of highway. He'd made his way past the section of lane closure, but the damage had been done. He was due in court half an hour ago.

His anxiety at his boss's reaction to his tardiness earned him a thorough search at the security checkpoint—making him even later than he already was. Great. Just fucking great. He took an extra second to adjust his tie and suitcoat, and to wipe a bead of sweat from his brow, before opening the courtroom door.

Jake had texted him that the judge had her own delays, and the proceedings had been pushed back a few minutes. He breathed a sigh of relief to see the judge's bench still empty. He hurried to the front of the room where Jake sat with the nervous couple eager to finalize the adoption of their first child.

"Sorry I'm late," he said, taking the chair between Jake and the couple. "Construction on the highway." He shook hands with his clients, bumped knuckles with the pint-sized adoptee, then retrieved a file from his briefcase then turned to his boss. "Jake, I can't thank you enough."

His boss held up a hand to stop him. "No thanks needed. However, we've got to get you a place in town. You're running yourself ragged commuting from Dallas, not to mention the cost of gas and your hotel room."

Brent nodded. "Jean has kept her eye on the real estate market for me. There's nothing available to rent or buy in Willowbrook." Truth. In their legal secretary's words, he'd better hope for someone to die. That was the only way something was going to come on the market. He wasn't that desperate. Yet. Though today's delay might push him over the edge. It was one thing to keep a client waiting in the office, another to be a no-show in court. Thank god, Jake was an understanding boss, but how much longer would his goodwill last?

"It's a tough market, that's for sure. We need some new construction in this town." Jake stood then nodded to the still-empty bench. "Since you're here now, I'll get on back to what I was doing." He congratulated the clients on what was a certain outcome of their petition to adopt then turned his attention back to Brent. "Can you meet me at the office Sunday around one? I think I might have a solution to your problem."

"Sure." Brent bobbed his head. "You got a spare closet I can put a cot in?"

Jake smiled. "No, but I might know someone who does."

With that, his boss strode confidently out of the courtroom, leaving Brent with a strange sense of foreboding. What the hell did he have in mind? There were literally no rooms available in Willowbrook.

The courtroom door closed behind his boss just as the judge entered at the other end, putting the kibosh on the questions running through Brent's mind. The entire proceeding took less than fifteen minutes then he was congratulating the new family. As he followed them out of the courthouse, he couldn't help but think how much better this job was, commute aside, than the one he'd had in Houston. When all you dealt with were corporations, you rarely saw how your work affected anyone. The new family walking ahead of him was visible proof his job had meaning.

Later today, he had a meeting with a young couple who were writing their first wills and wanted to establish trusts for their children. His expertise would help them provide for their children in the event something happened to one or both of them. No one liked to think in those terms, but planning for the unimaginable was wise. He liked being a part of the process, helping them to choose the right path for their family. The work wasn't as lucrative as being a corporate attorney, but it was a lot more satisfying. Since money wasn't one of his primary concerns, he welcomed the satisfaction his new job brought to his life.

Houston was in his rearview mirror, and, hopefully, Dallas soon would follow. He hadn't had much time to hang out in

Willowbrook, given his commute and the demands of his job, but what he had seen, he liked. The pace was slower. The people genuine and hardworking. The majority of the population had lived there all their lives. Some had spent time away but returned, like his boss. Jake had lived the big city corporate attorney life for several years before coming home to Willowbrook to take over his dad's law practice. Jake's brother, William, had lived the life of a celebrity artist in New York for years before moving back home. He'd come to the office a time or two to see Jake. Apparently, there were some unresolved legal issues from his time in New York. Jake had his hand in a few accounts, his brother's being top on his list. Thinking of his boss's family brought to mind the one Ingram brother Brent needed to stay far, far away from. Richard. The baby of the family but by no means a child. His brain, as it did anytime he thought of Rick Ingram, burst to life with images of the man.

His laugh when his brother's knees gave way when he saw his bride at the back of the church. His smile when he danced with his brother at the reception. The anguish in his voice when he implored Brent to keep his secret. The desire in his eyes when he pressed Brent against the hotel room wall. His sculpted torso when Brent wrestled his drunk body into bed. His naked ass when he drunkenly undressed in the middle of the night. His face relaxed in slumber the next morning.

The slideshow played on an endless loop, tormenting Brent in his loneliest moments. He'd gone back to the bar in Dallas several times, but the Adonis he'd flirted with that night must have been an out-of-towner. Other guys had flirted with him, but Brent wasn't interested. None of them looked like Rick Ingram. None of them were Rick Ingram.

And that was the crux of his current problem.

Only Rick Ingram would do.

~ ~ ~

As agreed, Brent met Jake on Sunday afternoon in the small parking lot behind Jake's law office in downtown Willowbrook. He'd spent the last few days wondering what his boss had up his sleeve. Their shared legal secretary, Jean, remained adamant there wasn't anything available for rent, not a house, not an apartment, not even a single room, in Willowbrook. Either Jake was a miracle worker, or he was full of shit. He hoped for miracle worker but was prepared for full of shit.

He waved as Jake pulled into the lot, came to a stop next to him, and rolled down the passenger side window. He leaned in. "Hey."

"Sorry to keep you waiting," Jake said, sweeping a leather portfolio off the passenger seat. "Hop in."

Brent dropped into the seat and reached for his seat belt. "I'm usually the one apologizing for being late."

His boss handed him the leather folder. "Sunny and I were going over some ideas. Lost track of time."

The slight color on his boss's cheeks led Brent to conclusions of his own about how Jake had lost track of time. He and Sunny were so newlywed, they were practically still on their honeymoon. "Not a problem, boss."

Jake shifted the car into gear and pulled out of the parking lot. He stopped at the stop sign marking the intersection half a block down. "I want you to do me a favor."

"What's that?"

A car crossed in the opposite direction then Jake accelerated through the intersection. "Keep an open mind today. And remember, if this works out, it's temporary."

Brent wanted something permanent, but for now, he'd take temporary. "How temporary?"

"Not sure. Six months, maybe? I'll know more in a bit."

It was on the tip of his tongue to ask what a bit was when Jake pulled to the curb in front of a small bungalow on a tree-shaded street within walking distance of everything downtown, including the law office. Brent's heart hammered. The white house resembled the others on the block but stood out because of the blue shutters. A wide walkway led from the sidewalk to a set of equally wide steps. Rocking chairs, abandoned for the winter, stood sentinel on a porch that spanned the front of the residence. He eyed the bushes across the front of the porch. Azaleas. He'd stake his life on it. Come spring, they'd put on a show with their bright blooms.

The house was exactly what he wanted for himself. "Is this place for sale?"

Jake grabbed the portfolio from Brent's lap then opened his door. "Nope."

He joined his boss on the sidewalk. "Rent?"

"Not the entire place."

He didn't care if the owner/occupant was a crazy cat lady/hoarder. He wanted to live there. Saw himself pushing a lawn mower over the lawn that would be green in a few more weeks. An empty flower bed bordering the driveway suggested bright annuals in springtime and through the summer months. His fingers itched to dig into the soil.

"You know the owner?" He followed Jake up to the porch.

Jake opened the screen door, placed his hand on the doorknob, and turned it. "You could say that."

What. The. Fuck?

Brent caught the screen before it hit him. Jake stepped inside. "Yo. Bro. What's up?"

Bro? Brent closed his eyes and prayed this was the home of the middle brother, Will. A familiar baritone met his ears. "Jesus, Jake. You scared the shit out of me. One of these days one of my idiot brothers is going to walk in on something you don't want to see."

"If only." Jake stepped aside, waving Brent into the room. "Since you're dressed and I don't see any sign of a woman, I think it's safe. I brought you some company."

"The Drillers are playing, Jake! This is my first day off since your wedding. Is it too much to ask to have a little privacy?"

Remaining mostly on the porch and out of sight, Brent tugged on Jake's jacket sleeve. Hoping to avoid detection, he pitched his voice low. "This isn't a good idea. I'm going to…go."

Jake whirled on him. "No. You need a place to live, and my dickhead brother has an extra room. So get your ass in here and let's talk." He tossed the portfolio on the coffee table, picked up the remote, and muted the television.

CHAPTER NINE

Brent reluctantly stepped over the threshold, keeping his eyes fixed on his feet, postponing a confrontation as long as possible. When he looked up and met Rick's gaze head-on, something sparked within him and grew into an all-consuming blaze in a matter of seconds. *Fuck!* He was in so much trouble.

"Jake?" Rick's voice sliced the air like a Marine Corps sword wielded by a master. "What's he doing here?"

God, that voice. Brent fought off the shiver racing down his spine. How would he ever survive hearing it on a daily basis?

"He needs a place to stay in town. The commute from Dallas is unacceptable. It's impacting his ability to do the job I hired him to do. There's nothing else available in this town or I wouldn't put you on the spot, but since Will moved in with Kenzie, you have an empty room."

Rick stood, walked away. Brent took the opportunity to admire his firm ass. He returned a moment later, a fresh beer in hand.

Jake paced around the room like he owned the place. "You work long hours. So does Brent. You'll hardly see each other. Did I mention it's a temporary situation?"

"How temporary?"

"Depends on how long it takes you to renovate his new apartment."

"What new apartment?" Brent and Rick asked at the same time.

Jake took a seat on the sofa, opened the portfolio. "The one above Sunny's new gallery, downtown."

Rick sat on one side of Jake. Curious, Brent sat on the opposite side. Jake twirled an architectural drawing around so they could all see it. "Sunny drew this up. It's not to scale or anything, just an artist's vision of the place. She needs some of the upstairs square footage for storage, but the rest we decided to convert into an apartment. We figured Brent could use it until something more to his liking comes on the market. After that, we'll use it as incentive to hire someone to operate the gallery so Sunny can spend more time with the baby."

Rick used a pointer finger to pull the rendering closer. "What about permits?"

"I've got friends at the planning commission. They're excited about bringing residential units to downtown. They're going to talk to some of the other building owners about converting their upper floors to rental units. If you can get this one done in a reasonable amount of time, it could generate a lot more business for you."

Rick lifted his chin at the stack of papers Jake had brought. "What else you got there?"

Jake fanned several sheets across the table. "Again, these aren't to scale, but you can see what Sunny has in mind. The actual apartment would be about twelve-hundred square feet.

She envisions two bedrooms, two bathrooms, and a galley kitchen." He pointed to a sketch of the living space. "She figures anyone she'd hire to run the gallery would probably be an artist themselves, so she wants to put in skylights and expand the windows on the front of the building to let in more light in case they want to use it as a studio."

"It's open concept. Have you had an engineer look at the structure to see if the existing walls can be taken down?"

Brent pulled one of the sketches closer while Jake and Rick talked engineering specs. Damn. Sunny had an eye for interior design. The place would be modern yet incorporated what he assumed was the existing charm of the old building. Anyone would be lucky to live there.

"Brent?" Jake elbowed him in the ribs. "What do you think? Can you put up with my brother for a few months while he builds an apartment for you?"

"Well." He swallowed hard then looked past his boss to meet the gaze of his potential landlord. "It would be temporary. Right?"

"It might be more than six months. Jake forgets I've got other obligations. Jobs I've already committed to, including his wife's gallery on the first floor of that building."

"Sunny's dealing with morning sickness, so putting the gallery renovation off is fine with her. Money's no object," Jake interjected. "Hire as many people as you need. Just get the job done. The sooner you do, the sooner Brent is out of your hair."

"I don't want to be a bother." Lord. He didn't want to live in the same house with Rick Ingram. But what choice did he have? Hoping for someone to die so he'd have a chance at a place to live wasn't just gruesome, it was unrealistic. About as unrealistic as keeping his hands off Rick. *But I will. I swear, I will.*

"It's no bother," Jake answered confidently for his brother. "Besides, one-third of this house belongs to me. As of right this minute, I'm claiming the spare bedroom and half the bathroom as mine and loaning it to Brent."

Rick jerked to his feet and paced away, his sexy-as-hell hand wrapped around his nape. He'd let his hair grow out some since the wedding. Brent longed to run his fingers through the too-long strands to see if they felt as soft as they looked.

Rick abruptly spun on his heel to face them. "He's paying rent. Enough to cover his share of the utilities, and he buys his own groceries." His gaze bored into Brent. "This isn't a social club. No dates. No sleepovers."

"Whoa." Jake stood to face off with his brother. "Just because you're antisocial doesn't mean your tenant has to be. He can bring anyone he wants over, and they can stay as long as they like."

Even though their arguing had an underlying tone of brotherly affection and hinted at years of similar negotiations, it was time to put an end to it. Brent stood. "I agree to Rick's terms. I don't have time for a social life anyway." The only person he wanted in his bed was Rick Ingram, and that wasn't going to happen, so no problem.

Rick glared at him. "Fuck." He shook his head then switched his gaze to Jake. "Okay. Okay, big brother. You win. I'll renovate the space, but you better clear the way with the permits. I want half up front to cover materials and hiring extra hands." He pointed a finger at Brent. "Stay the hell out of my way. You clean up your own messes." He named a reasonable rent.

Brent nodded. "Okay. First and last up front? I can draw up a rental agreement if you like."

"You lawyer types are fond of paper, so yeah, you write it up. I'll sign it. After my lawyer"—he cast a knowing glace at his brother—"reads it."

"Fuck, Rick." Jake shook his head. "I'll read the agreement, but I'm taking my fee out of your first payment."

"The fuck you are. You don't charge Will for legal services."

"Will *needs* a lawyer to look out for his interests. You don't."

It was a backhanded compliment—of sorts. The brothers stared at each other for the span of a couple of heartbeats then Rick found the remote under the scattered drawings. He resumed his place on the sofa and unmuted the game. "Fuck. The Drillers gave up two touchdowns. So much for making it to the championship game."

"That's our cue to leave." Jake gathered up his drawings then left without saying goodbye. Brent followed him out.

~~~

Rick kicked back in his new reclining sofa as the door closed behind his uninvited guests. What the fuck had he just agreed to? He'd just gotten Will out of his hair, and now that Brent guy was moving in?

He'd worked extra hours the day before to finish one job so he'd have one measly day off before starting the next job in the queue. Keeping busy had sustained him the three weeks since Jake's wedding, leaving him too exhausted to think about Dave's defection or the stupid mistake he'd made afterward. Working himself half to death had also kept him away from downtown Willowbrook, reducing the possibility of him running into Jake's new junior attorney—the keeper of Rick's
~~~

secret. Now the fucker was going to be his roommate. Slash that. Tenant. A paying guest. Nothing more.

A drop of cold water fell from the bottle he'd forgotten he still held. Since his drunken mishap after his brother's wedding, he hadn't allowed himself more than one bottle each night. This was what? His second today? He couldn't afford any more fuckups like that one. However, sobriety came with problems of its own, so he'd loaded his days to the max with work, hoping exhaustion would chase his demons away. When that didn't work, he invested in a set of weights and spent the restless hours in the middle of the night in the garage, lifting until his muscles screamed loud enough to drown out the memories. Surprisingly, it wasn't memories of Dave or of the way the man had broken his heart that kept him awake at night. The memory of emerald eyes behind nerd glasses fueled his late-night weightlifting sessions. Eyes filled with pity. Maybe a hint of amusement. Perhaps regret. Definitely hunger. He'd been drunk as the proverbial skunk that night, but he knew desire when he saw it. When he'd had Mr. Sin-in-a-suit pinned to the wall of that hotel room, glasses askew, he'd seen the flash of desire in his green eyes.

Bringing the bottle to his lips, he savored the cold, bitter taste. He'd discovered the Lucky Lady microbrewery a few towns over soon after his return to Willowbrook. The brewmaster had a sense of humor, assigning unique names to the brews in a way that reminded him of fortune cookies, and changing their flavors often. He had yet to find one he didn't like. This was the first from the six-pack he'd picked up last night, and from the taste of it, one he hadn't had before. He tilted the bottle so he could read the label. The emerald-green background reminded him of Brent's eyes. He shook off the ridiculous comparison and focused on the name of this particular brew. *Mistakes Make the Best Lovers.*

The laugh began as a chuckle deep in his gut, gained momentum the longer he looked at the label then burst forth in waves of mirth he couldn't contain.

Shit. I'm fucking doomed.

CHAPTER TEN

The following evening, Rick pinched the edges of a plastic tray, lifting the nuked meal from the microwave. "Shit. Fuck." He dropped the steaming TV dinner on the countertop with a *plop* then sucked the tip of his right pointer finger into his mouth. *Damn.* There had to be a better way to eat. He'd scalded the thumbs and forefingers on both hands on supposedly sealed entrees.

He'd just plunged his singed fingers under the cold tap when the doorbell rang. "Fuck." Shutting off the water, he hastily dried his hand, tossed the towel over the lip of the sink. The bell rang again just as he reached for the door handle. He yanked the door open, prepared to give whoever the hell it was a boot in the ass for interrupting his supper.

His new tenant, dressed to the nines in a tailored suit, stood on the porch surrounded by a shit-ton of suitcases. Rick's first thought was, *Fuck. I'd buy anything he's selling.* His second thought was, *Where the hell does he think all those clothes are going to go?*

Before he could voice either thought, Sin-in-a-suit grabbed the handle on the nearest roller bag with one hand and the screen door with the other. "You didn't give me a key."

Rick stepped back. "Don't need one. This is Willowbrook. I don't lock the door."

The newcomer dragged the first suitcase in then returned to the porch for another. Rick made no attempt to help him. Concierge wasn't part of his job description.

Brent retrieved the third case, an overstuffed garment bag, setting it on the floor at Rick's feet. "I've got expensive shit. Electronics, and sometimes I bring client files home. I'd appreciate it if we could lock up."

Rick shrugged. "There's a spare key in the bowl." He pointed to a green depression glass serving dish resting on a gateleg table behind the door. "Fits front and back locks. Just so you know, my brothers have keys, and, locked or not, they come and go as they please."

Brent huffed. "Yeah. Saw that for myself yesterday." He hefted a heavy case over the threshold. "Ever think of changing the locks?"

He had but didn't see the point. If Jake or Will wanted in, they knew all the secret ways to accomplish a break-in. Like the fact the window in what would be Brent's room wouldn't lock. "Nope," he said instead. "I repeat. This is Willowbrook. Crime rate—zero." He had cautioned Will and Kenzie to lock their doors. If Will's former fiancée came to town, they were more at risk there than anywhere else in town.

With the last of his wardrobe inside, Brent shut the door. Fuck, he was sexy as hell, even with his nose turned up, sniffing like a goddamn hunting dog.

"What's that smell?" He scrunched his face up like he was going to puke. "Tell me that's not something I'm going to have to get used to."

"Fuck you and the horse you rode in on." Rick left him standing in the living room. He called out from the kitchen, "Last door on the left is your room. Bottom drawer in the bathroom is yours."

He peeled the cellophane film off the top of his meal, grabbed a fork from the dish drainer, and dug in. A spewing sound, followed by a sickeningly overpowering floral smell made him forget all about the last of his meal, a brown brick that in no way resembled the brownie advertised on the meal's packaging. Rick spun around just as Brent entered the kitchen, what looked like a bug-bomb can held aloft as he sprayed chemicals into the air.

"What the fuck are you doing? Cut that shit out!"

Green eyes blinked behind those goddamn sexy glasses. He lowered his arm. He'd taken off his suit coat, rolled the sleeves of his white dress shirt halfway up his forearms, and loosened his tie. Rick's dick twitched to life. He did not want to be attracted to the guy, but fuck, he rocked the casual executive look.

"I will not live in a house that smells like a fart."

It was amazing the things grown men could find to amuse themselves at a remote desert outpost. Rick braced a hand on the counter, bent slightly at the waist, and squeezed out a fart guaranteed to startle any enemy combatants within a quarter mile radius. A championship winner if he ever heard one.

Brent stumbled back. "Oh, gross!" He waved a sheaf of papers in front of his face while directing a stream of flowery chemicals in Rick's general direction.

"Get used to it or get out. And for the love of god, quit spraying that shit everywhere."

"I'm not going anywhere, and I'll quit spraying when you quit fouling the air." He thrust the papers forward. "Here's the rental agreement. Sign it."

Rick lamented that his fart hadn't stunk. Just his luck. But he did get the satisfaction of rattling the lawyer, and damn, if that wasn't fun. He snatched the papers then sat at the small table where he'd eaten meals for most of his life. With just him living here, he rarely bothered to sit, preferring to eat at the counter. Looking at empty chairs around the table while he ate brought home just how much he missed having someone around. In the Marines, he'd never been alone.

Brent ventured closer until he stood over Rick's shoulder. "Just sign the last page. It's a standard rental agreement. Month to month since I don't know how long I'll need the room."

A check for the agreed-upon first and last month's rent was paperclipped to the top of the stack. Rick hesitated. This was his last chance to kick the man out and preserve his sanity. Once he signed the papers, lawyer in the family or not, he'd be stuck for at least six months with a tempting stranger who already knew too much about him. Probably longer.

"Jake looked it over. Call him if you don't believe me."

He'd already peeked at the last page and saw the Post-it Note from Jake that simply read, "Sign it." An arrow pointed to the line for his signature, like he was an idiot or something. Fuck Jake.

"Here. I brought a pen, just in case." Hot breath brushed his ear. A hand holding an expensive gold pen and a surprisingly muscular, masculine forearm appeared in his line of sight. Rick closed his eyes and stifled a groan as he imagined the sexy lawyer naked, strong arms encircling him from behind.

This was exactly why he shouldn't sign the document. The man had been in the house, what, ten minutes? And already Rick was thinking inappropriate thoughts. This was never going to work. Absolutely nothing good could come of touching the man. He had to make that clear.

The man behind him straightened. "Is that where the smell is coming from?"

Rick's gaze followed Brent's outstretched arm pointing to the frozen meal he'd almost finished eating. It did smell like shit and tasted little better, but it was fast and easy. He'd worked like the devil was on his heels today, cognizant that every minute wasted was another he'd have to endure this man's presence in his house. He'd been too tired to fix anything better for supper and too sweaty to pick anything up from the diner. Drive-thru fast-food joints had yet to find Willowbrook. "That smell was my supper. I know you're envious, but the frozen dinners in the freezer are mine. You want some, you buy your own."

Brent approached the counter like he expected the plastic tray to attack at any moment. He picked up Rick's abandoned fork and poked at the brownie brick. "You ate this? Man, you must have a cast-iron stomach."

Truth. Anyone who survived on MRE's for more than a day or two developed a thick stomach lining. He'd gone weeks with nothing but the Meals Ready to Eat for sustenance. "We've got more important things to discuss than my eating habits." He tapped the contract lying on the table.

"Like what?" His new tenant busied himself opening cabinets and drawers like he owned the place.

God, did he have to spell it out? "Like what happened after my brother's wedding."

Brent gently closed the cabinet beneath the sink before straightening to his full height. "What, exactly happened?"

Rick ran a hand over his jaw as he considered how much he wanted to tell this man. "Nothing," he said in conclusion. "You didn't see me after you left the reception. Period."

The man leaned his hips against the counter, arms crossed, eyes narrowed. "Okay. If that's what you want. How much do you remember about that night?"

"Not much."

"But you remember seeing me at the bar."

"Yeah. I vaguely remember you in my hotel room. Don't remember how we got there." He closed his eyes, briefly, as flashes of memory blasted through his brain. "You spent the night."

Brent nodded. "You were plastered. It wasn't safe to leave you alone."

"I didn't see any evidence of a condom." Heat rushed up his neck at the admission of just how plastered he'd been.

"That's because we didn't use one."

Rick groaned. His head dipped forward, too heavy for his neck. He rested an elbow on the table then dropped his forehead to his upturned palm. Laughter from across the room jolted him upright. Brent held his glasses in one hand while he dried his eyes with the other.

"You think we fucked?" He replaced his glasses. "Boy, you are so wrong." He chuckled. Pushing away from the counter, he opened the fridge, peered inside for a minute then helped himself to a beer. "Hope you don't mind. I'll replace it as soon as I can get to the store." He popped the top, took a long pull on the bottle then held it out to read the label. "This is some good shit. Where did you get it?"

"There's only one liquor store in town, dickwad. Where do you think I got it?"

Brent nodded then took another swig. "Okay. I'll buy you a six-pack. It was worth it to see the look on your face when you admitted you'd looked for a condom wrapper. You were too shitfaced to undress yourself, much less fuck." He relaxed against the counter. "I got most of your clothes off of you. Put you to bed then I made myself comfortable while you slept it off. I couldn't have lived with myself if I'd walked away then found out you'd choked on your own puke."

"I woke up naked."

"Not my fault. You woke up once. Enough to kick off your jeans and briefs then you went right back to sleep. I kinda thought for a minute you'd see me, maybe jump my bones, but you never even knew I was there."

Christ! Brent's words put more images in Rick's head, ones he now knew were pure fiction. Erotic fiction.

"You can thank me now."

Rick growled. Fuck. He did owe the man. God only knows what would have happened to him if someone else had coaxed him out of that bar. He hadn't been in any shape to say no or defend himself. He'd never been that fucked up in his life, and he never wanted to be again. He opened his mouth, but Brent cut him off before he could thank him.

"Nope. Don't bother. I don't need your thanks. How about you pay it forward? Help someone else out sometime. As for you and me, we met briefly at Jake's wedding and didn't see each other until yesterday when your brother sprang his downtown redevelopment plan on both of us."

Yeah. Rick nodded. "Okay." He half wished Brent wasn't such a decent guy. Maybe then he wouldn't entertain fantasies of unfastening those sexy trousers and sucking the man's cock between his lips—right here in the kitchen. "Pay it forward. I can do that." He picked up the pen he'd dropped and scribbled his name on the rental contract.

CHAPTER ELEVEN

It's self-preservation, Brent told himself as he stuffed papers into his briefcase in preparation for leaving the office earlier than usual. It was Friday night, and he'd have all weekend to read the pages Jean had typed up. He was tired of arriving home to find the entire house smelling like shit, thanks to Rick's obsession with frozen dinners. Tonight, he planned to beat his landlord home and prepare supper for both of them. He'd need to go to the grocery store first. Then make a stop at the liquor store for some wine and the six-pack he'd promised to purchase.

He couldn't understand why the man couldn't fix himself a decent meal. Brent loved the newly refurbished kitchen and couldn't wait to prepare an actual meal in it. So far, he'd existed on lunch meat, chips, and soda since he hadn't had time to shop for anything more elaborate. Tonight, he'd change that. He had a grocery list as long as his arm, and instead of walking to work, he'd driven so he could fill the trunk of his car with enough supplies to last the week. Since the rent he was paying was ridiculously cheap, he could afford to share a few meals with his landlord. Anything to keep those god-awful smells from permeating every room in the house.

He yanked the list from the inside pocket of his suit coat and added spray-on fabric deodorizer to the bottom. Jean had recommended the stuff. If it didn't work as advertised, he was going to have to have every one of his suits, ties, and dress shirts dry-cleaned to get the odors out. As an afterthought, he added plug-in air freshener to the list.

Outside, what had begun as a gloomy day had turned into a nightmare of freezing rain and slick streets, making him doubly glad he'd left the office early. The grocery store had been crazy crowded with people stocking up for a snowstorm rumored to be on the horizon, and since Brent didn't know his way around the aisles yet, the shopping had taken a lot longer than expected. To save time, he nixed the roast he'd planned on making, going with chicken alfredo, garlic bread, and a side salad instead. He'd just finished making the alfredo sauce from scratch when the back door swung open, letting in a blast of frigid air, followed by his sawdust-covered landlord.

"Whoa!" Brent held a hand up to stop the man from shedding his coat inches away from the pot of simmering sauce. "What do you think you're doing?" He shooed Rick back the way he'd come. "Shake that off outside, you moron. You'll ruin our dinner."

Rick glanced at the stovetop then his eyes traveled to the table set for two then back to Brent. "What the fuck?"

"Relax, macho man. It's not a date. It's food. You need it. I need it. Now get out of here until you're not a walking pigpen. Strip down outside then come in and get cleaned up. By the time you finish your shower, the pasta will be ready."

"You expect me to strip outside? It's fucking freezing!"

"At least shake all that…wait. Is that sawdust or snow?"

"It's snow, you idiot. Haven't you heard? They said to expect up to eight inches tonight."

Brent's gaze involuntarily dropped to Rick's crotch. Eight inches? Yeah. He'd caught a glimpse of the man's flaccid cock when he'd drunkenly shed his jeans and briefs that night. Aroused, he'd be every bit of eight inches. Brent swallowed hard and forced his gaze up to his pissed-off landlord's face. "Eight inches?" He turned to stir the sauce. "If you say so."

In his peripheral vision, he saw the man shed his coat and run a hand through his hair. He stomped his boots on the mat. "I was talking about snow, but as for my dick, you'll have to take my word for it, because I wouldn't show it to you if you were the last person on the planet and fucking you would bring back the species."

An image of the unlikely scenario bloomed in his brain. A shiver raced down his spine and straight to his balls. His dick rose to attention. *Shit.* He couldn't let Rick see how his words affected him. He was Jake's brother, for crying out loud. Not to mention, he didn't want to be thrown out on his ass for sexually harassing his landlord—especially when he was at the mercy of said landlord to finish his new apartment. He gave the sauce another stir then because it allowed him to keep his back to his landlord, he crossed to the retro refrigerator for the butter and fresh herbs he planned to spread on the Italian baguette he'd picked up in the bakery department.

"Ditto, macho man." He didn't know what made him say it, but the words were out of his mouth before he could stop them. "You had your chance, but you were too shitfaced to follow through. Your loss."

The air stirred behind him as Rick clomped through the kitchen. Brent inhaled deeply, taking in the fresh scent of the outdoors, and the heady musk of sexy male the man left behind. His cock pressed insistently against the zipper of his jeans. Brent closed the fridge door then leaned his forehead against it. *I'm soooo fucked.*

~ ~ ~

Rick couldn't get out of the kitchen fast enough. Despite the threat of snow and ice, or maybe because of it, he'd put in extra hours on his current project and had anticipated coming home to an empty house as he'd done all week long. He thought he put in long hours, but Brent surpassed him, leaving early in the morning, and not returning until Rick was in bed. He'd hear the man in the kitchen, fixing himself something to eat before he, too, went to bed, but not once had the man actually *cooked* anything.

The cozy scene, complete with delicious smells wafting from pots on the stove, nearly knocked him on his ass. Then he'd caught sight of Brent, and he'd lost the ability to breathe. The man oozed sex appeal in his lawyer gear, but put the man in jeans, a Henley, and an apron, and fuck! Thank god, Brent had lit into him because he had been ten seconds or less from pushing the man up against the refrigerator and kissing the fuck out of him.

He cranked the shower all the way to hot, stripped down then stepped under the spray. The new heating system for the house he was working on wouldn't be installed until next week and the old one barely worked. He'd been fucking freezing his ass off all day long. Then he'd walked in, and his internal temperature had spiked, and his frozen dick had surged to life. Why couldn't the bastard have worked late tonight? Gotten snowed in at the office? Left him the fuck alone?

Rick lifted his face to the hot spray and willed his erection to go the fuck away. Like everyone else in his life, it refused to listen to reason. Brent wasn't his. Wasn't going to be his. Wasn't even his type. If he had a type.

He'd only had one serious relationship in his entire adult life, and he could count the number of sexual partners he'd had on one hand. The only one he'd known well enough to classify as a type had been Dave, and he qualified as the polar opposite of the man standing in Rick's kitchen looking like a fucking celebrity chef in his designer jeans and cashmere sweater.

It was like zero-fucking degrees outside, and the man was barefoot. Barefoot! Why he'd noticed the man's feet, and why their state of undress bothered him, he didn't want to examine. Just another fucking reason he had to get Brent out of his house sooner rather than later. Get him out before he drove him stark, fucking mad.

Willing his mind to focus on something else, Rick took a deep breath. His lungs filled with warm, moist air heavily laden with the scent of Brent's high-end body wash that smelled nothing like his plain-label discount store brand. His abdominal muscles clenched, and his balls drew up tight. Bracing one hand on the tiles he'd installed last summer, he grabbed his straining dick with his free hand and stroked. Once. Twice. He didn't even try to fight the fantasy brought on, apparently, by lack of oxygen to his brain, for there could be no other reason for imagining his roommate, bare-assed and bent over the kitchen table while Rick fucked him into next week.

He took his time dressing. The images his addled brain had conjured up in the shower had yet to fully dissipate. Christ, he had no business fantasizing about the man. Under no circumstances would he become sexually involved with Brent.

He didn't know for sure, but he assumed, since he'd seen him in a gay bar in Dallas, that his brother's new employee wasn't hiding his sexuality in the closet. If he was going to hook up with someone, they'd have to be as circumspect as he. Which meant, if he was going to have sex with anyone other than his own hand, he'd have to go out of town to do it. If an enclave of gay men existed in Willowbrook, he sure as hell hadn't heard about it. Even if he had, he wouldn't trust them to keep his secret. The gossip grapevine in this town worked better than the telephone system. Always had.

When he'd stalled as long as he thought he could without raising suspicion, he pulled on a pair of socks, because there was something about bare feet that suggested a certain level of intimacy, and made his way to the kitchen. Brent, his glasses slightly askew, spun around. He hastily righted the eyewear then wiped his palms on the front of his apron.

"There you are." His smile reminded Rick of the way the Afghani villagers smiled at his team when they walked through their towns, weapons at the ready and in full battle gear. Their smiles would be strained, cautious, as if they weren't sure if they should welcome the newcomers or not. "I was afraid I was going to have to mount a search party." Brent lifted a giant saucepan from the stove. "Much longer and the pasta would be paste." He dumped the creamy sauce over an enormous platter of noodles.

"Have a seat." He rinsed the saucepan in the sink. "I didn't know what kind of salad dressing you liked, so I got a couple of different kinds."

Rick eyed the row of bottles on the table. "You didn't have to do this." But, damn, the kitchen smelled amazing, and after eating nothing but frozen meals for weeks, the fresh salad greens were tempting. He picked up the bottle of creamy ranch dressing.

Brent hefted the platter of sauce and noodles into the center of the table. Before taking his seat at the opposite end of the small table, he removed the apron and hung it from one of the cabinet knobs. "It wasn't any trouble." He poured a vinaigrette over his own salad. "I would have done it sooner, but I needed to take off work early to go to the store. He tossed his head toward the door. "Good thing I made the effort today, or we'd be stuck here all weekend with nothing but a dwindling supply of frozen meals and a stale jar of peanut butter."

Rick glanced out the window over the sink as he munched on a bite of crisp greens. The snow was coming down hard, creating a veil of white outside. "I usually stock up on Saturday. Looks like that'll have to wait this week."

"I bought plenty of food. It should keep starvation from our door until they get the roads cleared or this stuff melts off."

Rick brought his focus to the meal in front of him. "I'll pay you for my share."

He'd never seen the napkin-lined basket Brent held out to him. "Garlic bread. Since we won't be getting physically close, I went heavy on the garlic." Rick selected a perfectly browned slice of bread topped with garlic, butter, and cheese then Brent set the basket in front of his plate. "Consider the groceries, and the meal, a thank-you gift. I can't tell you how much easier my life has been this week. The commute was killing me, and lord, how I hate living out of a suitcase."

Rick scooped a generous helping of pasta onto his plate and dug in. A symphony of flavors burst on his tongue. He hummed his appreciation before swallowing. Shit, the man could cook. Digging his fork in for another bite, Brent's words registered. He recalled the giant suitcases the man had brought with him. "What did you do with all your clothes?"

The closet in that bedroom was tiny. Clothes, shoes, toys, and sporting gear belonging to the three boys who grew up in the room had perpetually tumbled from the sorry excuse for storage. No way would the closet hold even half of Brent's wardrobe.

"Um." His roommate twirled cream-drenched noodles around his fork. "I was going to speak to you about that. Is there another closet I could use? And I could use another dresser, too, though I don't know where I would put it."

Rick had removed the bunk beds they'd slept in as kids and replaced them with a full-sized bedframe. That hadn't left room for anything more than a small dresser and mirror. He probably should have offered to switch rooms with him since everything he owned fit in a couple of drawers, leaving the large closet in his bedroom nearly empty, but this was his house and he hadn't asked for a roommate. Still.

He sighed and dropped his fork. Fuck. The man had cooked for him, and he hadn't uttered a single complaint since he'd moved in. He wasn't even complaining about the lack of storage in his room, he was just pointing it out. Politely.

Rick took a sip of the wine Brent had insisted he try. He preferred beer, but the crisp white tasted pretty damn good. He took another sip then placed his glass on the table, spinning the stem between his thumb and forefinger. The glass itself was a new addition since Rick had never bothered to purchase any, and if his parents had ever owned any, they had long since been broken or perhaps donated to the church rummage sale after their mother's passing.

He cleared his throat. "The closet in my bedroom is a lot bigger, and it's almost empty. You can hang some of your stuff in there if you want. You can store your suitcases in the garage.

Since Will moved out, there are a few empty shelves along the back wall."

Brent set his fork on the edge of his plate and reached for his wineglass. "I don't want to inconvenience you. I can make do. I was thinking of getting one of those rolling clothes racks. I could hang my shirts on it and save the sturdier rod in the closet for the heavier suits." He sipped his wine. "I appreciate the offer though." He eyed Rick over the rim of his glass. "This can't be easy for you."

Rich shrugged. "I grew up in this house." Remembering what it was like, he snickered. "I shared the room you're in with two older brothers. I never knew what peace and quiet was until I'd been in the Marines a couple of years and moved off base. Deployment was a lot like three teenagers sharing a tiny room, only we had guns, so we tried to stay in our space and not piss off our roommates." He shoved a forkful of pasta in his mouth and chewed, washing it down with more wine. "You're quieter than Will, and you can cook. My brother *thinks* he can cook, but trust me, he can't, so if you want the closet space, it's yours."

Brent topped off Rick's wineglass. "How about this? I'll accept the closet space, and in return, I'll cook dinner during the week. We can save our eating out for the weekends."

Rick envisioned the crappy frozen dinner he'd be eating tonight if Brent hadn't shared the meal he'd cooked. He didn't relish the idea of the man parading through his room to get to the closet, but damn, he'd be a moron to pass up homecooked meals while the guy was here. He nodded. "Okay, but I'll pay my half of the grocery bill and do the dishes. If something comes up and you can't cook, just let me know and I'll nuke a TV dinner or pick up something at the diner."

Terms agreed upon, they ate in silence. When he was done, Brent took his plate to the sink. "You're sure you're okay doing the dishes?"

Rick eyed the mess and nodded. He'd cleaned up worse. "I'm good." He waved his fork at the remains on the table. "Thanks again."

Brent nodded then pushed away from the counter. "I'm going to sort some clothes. I'll put the things I don't wear as often in your closet. That way I won't be going in and out of your room as often."

Rick finished off the noodles on his plate. "Yeah. That sounds like a good idea."

"I'll leave you to it, then."

Rick remained in his seat after Brent left, willing his dick to behave. Sharing a meal with Brent was pure torture. The man's appreciative sounds when he'd tasted his food were enough to drive a man to drink. Watching his tongue sweep over his lips to capture every stray bit of creamy sauce had Rick so hard, it was a wonder he'd been able to carry on even a half-coherent conversation. Which probably accounted for him offering closet space to the man.

What the hell had he been thinking? The trouble was, he knew exactly what he'd been thinking, and it involved his dick, a different creamy substance on Brent's lips, and that tongue. God almighty, that tongue, licking, teasing, making him see stars. He'd imagined Brent on his knees, wearing his lawyer gear, his glasses magnifying pleading eyes as Rick fucked his mouth.

The sound of a door closing down the hall forced Rick from his X-rated musings. Swiping a sweaty hand over his face, he blew out a frustrated breath. Gathering the bottles of salad dressing, he took them to the refrigerator then stood, letting the chilled air cool his heated skin. This was all Jake's fault. His big brother would pay for putting him through this torture.

CHAPTER TWELVE

Brent collapsed on the bed, face-first, one hand gripping his throbbing erection while he bit down on the other to stifle the frustrated moans burning his throat.

Living in the same house with Rick Ingram was the worst decision he'd ever made in his life. Worse than taking Cynthia Prendergast to the prom and fighting off her wandering hands all night long. Worse than hooking up with that football player his first semester at the University of Texas. Worse than trading a blow job for a well-written paper on *Pride and Prejudice*, even if it did mean the difference between passing or failing Classic Lit. He'd only taken the class because the sexy nerd he was crushing on at the time, ultimately the recipient of the blow job, convinced him he would love the class. Deciding to live with Rick Ingram even topped screwing the proctor of his LSAT session. Granted, he hadn't known the guy would proctor his exam at the time. They'd met at an Austin bar, fucked in the bathroom then, mutually satisfied, parted ways. Brent had been shocked when he'd arrived at the test site the next day and found the guy sitting at the proctor's desk. The tests were all online these days, so there couldn't have been even a hint of fuck-to-pass going on, but still. It wasn't something he wanted anyone to know. Just in case.

He had no one to blame but himself—and maybe Jake Ingram—for his current predicament. Maybe he'd let Jake off the hook. His boss couldn't have predicted Brent would do something so stupid. He'd offered to cook for a man who made him hard just by breathing. And, he'd traded that torture for what was sure to be even more torture.

Walking past Rick's bed. Imagining rumpled sheets that smelled like Rick made his dick even harder. There was no hope for it, he was going to have to ease his own suffering like he'd done every night since he'd moved in, and most mornings, too. He'd spilled more spunk over Rick Ingram in one week than on any man he'd ever been with, including Kenneth. He didn't care to examine what that said about his former relationships. Instead, he rose to his knees and whipped off his shirt. After spreading it on the comforter, he unbuttoned the fly on his jeans and shoved them and his boxers down to mid-thigh. Bracing himself on one outstretched arm, he took his aching cock in hand and, closing his eyes, imagined the shirt beneath him was a certain former Marine. In a matter of minutes, he came, shooting ribbons of hot cum onto his phantom lover.

~ ~ ~

The unnatural silence woke Rick early. He lay in bed for a few minutes listening for the usual sounds that heralded the coming of a new day. Nothing. Not a bird chirping. No cars driving by. Even the house had settled in, refusing to creak its old bones.

He threw the covers off and swung his feet to the floor. "Fuck!"

He really needed to buy a rug for his room. The original hardwood floors in these old pier and beam houses were trendy but cold as fuck in the winter. Grabbing the socks and sweatpants he'd tossed to the end of the bed when he'd crawled beneath the covers the previous night, he hurriedly dressed then eased the door open. He crossed the hall to the shared bathroom, did his business then ambled to the kitchen.

The scene out the living room window stopped him cold. Cold being the operative word. Blinking, he approached the scene with caution. Beyond the plate-glass window, a heavy blanket of snow covered everything like frosting on a fancy cake. A layer of gray clouds filtered the rising sun, adding shadows to the already surreal landscape. *I wonder if Will is seeing this.* His artist brother wasn't a morning person, but for this, he needed to make an exception. Rick extracted his phone from the pocket of his sweatpants, clicked a couple of photos, and sent them in a text message to Will.

"It's beautiful, isn't it?"

The words, spoken softly over his right shoulder, startled him. Rick spun, his fists at the ready. His bare-chested roommate, hands up in surrender, backpedaled.

"Whoa. It's just me, Marine. I heard you moving around. Thought I'd come see what the day has in store for us." He waved at the scene beyond the window. "Didn't expect anything like that."

Rick blew out a breath as his gaze took in the man's disheveled state. His usually impeccably groomed hair looked sinfully mussed. The shadow of a beard, several shades darker than his hair, shadowed his jaw. Rick curled his hands into fists as the need to reach out and touch washed over him. He forced his gaze lower. *Shit.* For a lawyer, Brent was fit as fuck. Defined. That was the word. Every muscle from his shoulders to the carved V disappearing beneath his low-slung pajama pants was delineated to perfection. God. Fucking. Damn.

He faced the winter wonderland, silently cursing Mother Nature's wicked sense of humor. The city of Willowbrook didn't own snow removal equipment. Never had. So, until the sun came out and melted all that fucking snow, he was housebound with a man he wanted more than he wanted his next breath. He'd normally thank the universe for such a problem, but since the man in question was off-limits, he was fucking screwed.

"Well, I didn't hear you. Make some fucking noise in the future." He hoped the emotion in his voice conveyed anger rather than arousal, but he couldn't be sure.

Brent stepped up so they stood facing the window, bare shoulder to bare shoulder. Rick took a slow, deep breath, willing his libido to stand down. His gaze glazed over as Brent's clean scent wafted on the warm air rising from the floor register near their feet.

"How long before they plow the road?"

Rick huffed out a laugh. "The only plows around here are for dirt, city boy."

"Wait. What? You mean no one is going to clear the streets today?"

Rick groaned and rubbed both palms over his face. He needed coffee. Lots of it. He stumbled into the kitchen. "That's what I'm sayin'. Unless you want to walk in that, you're stuck here for a while."

Brent followed him into the kitchen. "How long?" He retrieved a container of cream from the refrigerator while Rick popped a single-serve pod into the coffee maker then slid his favorite mug beneath the spout.

Rick leaned against the counter as the life-giving brew dripped into his mug. "Why? You got someplace to go?"

"No. I was just wondering."

Fuck. He'd hoped Brent had something important to do today. Something that would take him out of the house and keep him out. "Well, to answer your question—how long depends on the weather. I've never seen this much snow before, but if the sun comes out, the roads should be passable tomorrow. If this cloud cover hangs around and the temperature doesn't get above freezing, then the snow isn't going anywhere. There's already a layer of ice beneath all the white stuff. If the snow starts to melt and the temperature drops again, the layer of ice will only get worse."

His roomy rested one hip against the counter, crossed his muscular arms over his chest, his gaze fixed on the brown liquid filling Rick's mug. "They'll treat the ice, right?"

"Eventually. They'll salt and sand the intersections and the main roads." He cocked his head toward the front of the house. "We're not on a main road."

When the coffee maker spit out its last drop, Rick took his mug to the table and sat to savor the first few sips. Brent replaced the spent coffee pod with a new one then slid a fresh mug under the spout. "I guess this means you won't be going to the job site today."

Rick shook his head. "I should, but I'm not." He had no doubt his pickup could handle the snow. It was the layer of ice beneath that made driving tricky. He'd seen it too many times growing up. People didn't see the fluffy white stuff as a threat. They'd get out on the roads and end up in a ditch somewhere because of the hidden ice. He'd just have to work longer hours to make up for the lost time. He took a sip of his coffee. "Don't worry. I'm on track to start work on your apartment week after next, as planned."

Brent added cream to his coffee before joining Rick at the table. "I'm not worried about the apartment. If you need to put it off to take care of your other customers, that's okay with me."

The man's offer brought Rick up short. He locked gazes with his roommate. "I thought you were in a hurry to have your own place."

"I was. I mean, I am." Brent raised his mug to his lips but didn't drink. "I like it here. This kitchen is a dream, and I fell in love with the house before I knew it was yours. It's exactly the kind of place I was hoping to find, but I quickly learned the error of my ways. So"—he sipped his coffee—"the apartment over the gallery will have to do."

Rick dropped his gaze to his almost-empty mug. *Fuck.* He needed something stronger than coffee, but the last thing he needed was alcohol clouding his judgement while he was stuck in the same house with Brent. He still couldn't recall everything that happened after Dave dumped him on the evening of Jake's wedding. Snatches of memory had come back to him, some more clear than others. However, the one he recalled with the most clarity was the one he most wanted to forget. Thank god, he'd been too soused to follow through on his desire, or he would have fucked his brother's new employee up against the hotel room wall then drilled him into the mattress for good measure.

Yeah, the sooner he got Brent out of his house, the better. "I'll get the apartment done for you as soon as possible."

The man nodded then pushed up from the table. "How about pancakes? I've been dying to make them ever since I saw you had a gas range." Without waiting for Rick's reply, he pulled supplies from the cupboards. "They're almost impossible to do on an electric range. Too much temperature variation."

He rambled on, but Rick couldn't hear for the blood rushing past his ears on its way south. He'd never seen a man in pajama pants before. The four males growing up in his household had slept in briefs, and the Marines sure as hell didn't issue sleepwear. Stateside, Dave had slept nude, and Rick had developed the same habit. Made things easier, he figured. He'd pulled on the sweats this morning to keep his dick from shriveling in the cold. He should have known better. Anytime Brent was around, Rick's blood ran hot, and his dick was anything but shriveled.

Damn, cotton plaid should not look sexy, but it fucking did on Brent. Rick couldn't drag his gaze away from the man's ass shifting beneath the thin material or the way the elastic waistband sat low on his hips, revealing two perfect dimples.

Fuck pancakes. Rick desperately wanted to taste those indentations—and more. Stifling a groan, he stood. "I'm going to get dressed." *Right after I strangle the snake.*

"Take your time," Brent singsonged, oblivious, apparently, to Rick's distress.

As soon as Rick's ass disappeared from view, Brent collapsed. Elbows braced on the kitchen counter, he cradled his head in his upturned hands. "Fuck. Fuck. Fuck." He whispered the words to the granite countertop. Two whole days, maybe more, stuck in the house with Rick Ingram. "Just kill me now."

Forcing himself upright, he gripped his raging hard-on through the soft flannel of the pajama pants he'd put on for the sake of decency before joining Rick to survey the snowy landscape. He'd like to pass his erection off as morning wood, but lying to himself wasn't going to help his situation. He'd gone from morning wood to painful steel the second he'd seen Rick standing in the living room, wearing those god-awful white socks, well-worn Marine Corps sweats, and nothing else. It was enough to make a grown man weep with gratitude for being alive. And curse the day he was born.

"Repeat after me. I will not fuck with Rick Ingram." He huffed out a breath then grabbed the wire whisk and took out his frustration on the pancake batter. "I like my job. I like my boss. I like Willowbrook. I will *not* fuck this up." His hand cramped from the strangle hold he had on the whisk. Easing his grip, he tapped the tool on the edge of the bowl to release the batter from the tines. He might have overdone it with the mixing, but he couldn't find it within himself to give a fuck.

Earlier in the week, he'd found a cast-iron griddle in one of the cabinets. He dug it out and placed it on the stovetop. While he waited for it to heat, he opened the new syrup bottle he'd purchased and unwrapped a stick of real butter. None of that fake stuff. Maybe the flavor would make up for overmixing the batter. He turned the first pancake too early then left it too long on the flipside, so it ended up looking like an ink blob. The second one was better, and by the third, he had the timing down and had established a rhythm. Pour. Flip. Scoop. Pour again. He was in the process of pouring batter on the hot griddle when Rick came back in wearing a long-sleeved T-shirt that might have been spray-painted on, faded jeans worn paper thin in all the right places, and paint-splattered work boots. Proving once and for all, it didn't matter what the man did or did not wear, he was sexy as fuck. He hadn't bothered to shave, the thick, dark stubble coupled with his still sleep-tussled hair added a whole new level to his macho-man appearance.

"Whoa." He signaled to the sizzling pan. "Better watch what you're doing."

"Huh?"

"The griddle?"

Yeah. The griddle. Brent snapped his gaze to the iron square. "Shit!" A giant blob of pancake batter oozed toward the edge on all sides. He righted the ladle, but it was too late. If he managed to salvage it, he'd have a pancake the size of a hubcap on a 1950 Cadillac.

Rick chuckled as he reached past Brent to get a plate from an upper cabinet. Using his fingers, he helped himself from the stack warming on the stove. "These look fantastic. Thanks."

Brent kept his back to the man. Rick's chuckle when he'd seen the mess Brent had made suggested he knew he'd caused the mishap to occur. Damn sex bomb. There should be a law against looking as good in clothes as out. Brent concentrated on the mess he'd created and did his best to tune out the sounds of gastronomic pleasure coming from the kitchen table. Bubbles popped in the center of the massive flapjack, and the edges were firming. He'd need to flip it or dump it soon. Dumping it meant admitting, unequivocally, that he'd made a mistake. No way was he acknowledging how much Rick affected him. So, flipping it was.

He dug in the drawer where he'd found the spatula he was using, hoping to find another but came up empty-handed. He could try to toss the cake in the air like he'd seen professional chefs do, but lifting the cast-iron griddle by itself was difficult. Doing it weighted down with a giant glob of batter would be impossible.

"Need help with that?" Rick stood beside him, his gaze fixed on the raw hubcap.

"I need to turn it but can't figure out how," he admitted.

"I've got an idea." His roomy took a plate from the cabinet then returned to stand beside him. "You lift the edge. I'll slip the plate underneath and lift it off the griddle. Then all we have to do is flip it over, and *voila*! Problem solved."

It sounded like it would work. Brent nodded. "Okay. Let's give it a try."

He slid the spatula beneath the front edge and carefully lifted it away from the griddle. He stepped back as far as he could to allow Rick room to edge in and slide the plate underneath the half-baked mess. He got about halfway when the whole thing began to slide. Instead of stopping, he made a last-ditch effort to scoop the mass onto the plate. And it worked.

"Ta-da!" He held the plate aloft, his grin one Brent was sure his brothers had seen many times growing up, one that said *I told you I could do it*. "Now, to flip it onto the griddle."

Immediately realizing Rick's error, Brent cried out, "No!" But it was too late, the plate was already moving, flipping like a flying saucer doing tricks for an alien airshow. The gooey hubcap fell, landing with a sickening splat on the griddle. Raw batter splashed out in every direction, coating everything in its path with sticky goo.

Plate still in hand, Rick's gaze met Brent's then his eyes dropped lower. Brent followed his gaze to the streaks of batter slowly dripping down his bare torso. If a person didn't know it was pancake batter, he might think it was something else. Brent groaned. He lifted his gaze to Rick's. What he saw in the other man's eyes froze the breath in his lungs. Heat. Hot enough to fry brain cells. "Rick." His voice sounded scorched, like he'd downed a bottle of pepper sauce with a vinegar chaser. On the stovetop, batter sizzled, and steam escaped in hiccups from the remains of the hubcap.

Slowly, Rick bent. His tongue darted out, capturing a long, thin line of batter before it slid beneath the waistband of his pajama pants. Brent gasped. A shiver ran down his spine and gooseflesh pebbled his arms where he held them rigid at his sides.

"Mmm." Another tongue swipe. "Tastes good."

"Rick."

Another lick. "Hmm?"

"We…can't." A hand shot to his waist, holding him steady. Another tongue lashing, this one over his right nipple. His eyes rolled back in his head as he fought the urge to wrap his arms around Rick's head and hold him there. Force him to suck his nipple. Beg him to do that and so much more. "We…shouldn't."

Rick straightened, breaking all bodily contact. Brent closed his eyes and bit his lower lip, holding in a plea he had no business uttering. *Good. I got through to him.* He let out a pent-up breath. Recalling his earlier determination to keep his employers' baby brother at arm's length, he mentally congratulated himself on putting a stop to certain disaster. But it had been a close call. One more lick. One more touch, and he wasn't so sure he could or would have said anything.

Click.

Brent popped his eyes open. His gaze flew to the burner control knob, now in the Off position, to the man standing between him and the stove. Okay, he mentally nodded. Safety first. Turning the burner off was a good move. Then both Rick's hands were on his waist, hauling him forward until he collided with a solid wall of muscle. Holy fuckarama. It was like Rick's body was a giant electromagnet and Brent had become steel. He was trapped, immobilized by an attraction as strong as it was invisible.

"Look at me."

CHAPTER THIRTEEN

They were nearly the same height, but the thick soles of his work boots gave him a slight advantage over Brent's bare feet. How he'd ever thought clothes made of ordinary cloth would be sufficient armor against Brent's allure was beyond comprehension. From the moment he'd met him at Jake's wedding, desire for the man had been festering inside him like a fatal disease on the march. He'd kept it at bay with thoughts of Dave. Of being with Dave. But with that barrier shattered, the only thing standing between Rick and his lust was his brother, and he'd be damned if Jake controlled his sex life. As long as Brent was consenting, there wasn't any reason they couldn't fuck themselves into a coma if they wanted. No one outside these walls had to know.

"Look at me," he repeated.

Slowly, Brent lifted his chin. Their gazes locked. "This is insane." The words were nothing more than a whisper.

"Fuck, yeah, it's insane. But I'm tired of fighting it. I want you, and you want me."

Brent remained silent. His eyelids dropped, breaking their connection. His hands fisted at his sides.

"Tell me I'm wrong. Say you don't want me, and I won't touch you again." His patience and his control were slipping. He framed Brent's face with his hands, brushed the man's tight lips with his own. "Maybe you need to hear what I'm going to do to you." Brent's whimper was the cue to proceed Rick needed.

Bending his head, he whispered in his ear. "I'm going to force you to your knees and shove my cock down your throat until your eyes water and you beg me to shove it up your ass. Then I'm going to lay you out on my bed, face-first, and ream your ass so hard, you won't be able to sit for a week." He licked the shell of his ear. Brent shivered but made no effort to move. "Then I'm going to flip you over so I can see your face when I fill you with my cum."

Rick nipped at his earlobe. "And, if you're good and don't come before I tell you, you know what I'll do?"

"What?" If his ear hadn't been an inch from the man's lips, he wouldn't have caught the softly spoken word. But he *had* heard him.

Rick was ready to explode. He'd sped right past the friendly roommates' signpost long ago and had arrived at the final exit on the road to insanity marked, dirty, filthy fuckbuddy. "I'll tell you what," he growled. Speaking low, directly into the man's ear, Rick spelled it out for him. "I'll take your dick in my hot, wet mouth and suck you like a fucking industrial Hoover until you come so hard, they'll see it from the International Space Station and think there's a new geyser on the planet."

He paused to let the man get his breathing under control. "Nod if you want me to do all those things to you or step away now, while I still have the ability to let you go."

Rick had waited hours, sometimes days, for the enemy to make a move, to give away their position, but none of that waiting compared to the excruciatingly long seconds it took for Brent to make up his mind. When the man slowly sank to his knees, it took Rick's brain a moment to catch up. His own words echoed in the space formerly occupied by his brain. *I'm going to force you to your knees and shove my cock down your throat until your eyes water and you beg me to shove it up your ass.*

Grabbing a fistful of the man's hair, Rick dragged his head back. A gasp escaped Brent's parted lips. God, those lips. A fresh supply of blood rushed to Rick's cock in anticipation of fucking that mouth. Orbs as green as spring leaves, clear behind nerdy glasses, peered up at him. Like any enemy combatant facing the reality of failure, Brent's eyes held contempt, for himself, for the overwhelming force—in this case, desire—he couldn't defeat. Deeper still, lay relief. Relief that the battle was over. Won or lost, it didn't matter. War exhausted a man, physically and mentally. Like Rick, Brent had been at war with his desires, his needs. Rick had surrendered to his desires and forced the final battle between them. To the victor goes the spoils. "You agree to my terms of surrender?"

Brent trembled with his answer. "Yes. God damn you, yes."

With his one hand still fisted in Brent's hair, Rick worked his belt loose with the other. In the snow-cloaked silence, the jingle of his belt buckle sounded as loud as mortar rounds. Sucking in his stomach, Rick slid his zipper down. Keeping his gaze locked with Brent's, Rick reached in, dragged his balls and engorged dick through the opening.

"Hands behind your back," he commanded.

With a growl, Brent complied.

Rick fisted his other hand in the man's hair then forced his face down. "Open your mouth."

Brent opened for him.

Rick flexed and shimmied, teasing those perfect lips with the head of his cock. He'd been leaking precum since his first taste of the man's batter-splattered skin. He loved the way his secretions looked slicked over Brent's lips. A mark of possession. When he couldn't stand it any longer, he shoved his cock past Brent's lips until the man gagged on the head of his cock and his balls tapped his chin. Gripping Brent's head tight between his palms, Rick commanded, "Suck me like your life depends on it."

~ ~ ~

Every survival instinct he had urged Brent to fight back. To unclasp his hands and shove the man away. To scramble to his feet and run fast and hard as far away from Rick Ingram as he could get. But he didn't. His eyes watered and his nose ran as he gagged on the man's enormous cock. Another instinct had his lips closing over the wide girth. He forced air in through his nostrils then swallowed. The move earned a curse from his tormentor who pulled his cock almost all the way out then shoved it deep again. And again. And again. Tears ran from Brent's eyes, and he fought for every breath. Spit leaked from his abused lips and coated the steel shaft relentlessly fucking his mouth.

Rick's hands clamped his head like a vise as he grunted and cursed and brutalized his mouth. A hate fuck. Brent hated it almost as much as he loved it. He *hated* that he loved it. Hated that he *wanted* it. Hated that he *needed* it. Hated that Rick knew all those things about him. Yet, Brent loved that Rick felt all those things as well. He loved that Rick had caved to their mutual desire first. The big, bad Marine broke.

Or maybe he was just broken.

A hole opened in Brent's heart at the thought of Rick alone and suffering the way he had been, following his brother's wedding. The man had grown adept at hiding his true self, but that night, and right now, he dropped the walls he'd built and allowed Brent to see him. No doubt, he'd extract another vow of silence when he came to his senses, and Brent would reluctantly grant it. Owning your sexuality was something every person had to come to on their own time in their own way. He'd been lucky. His family loved and accepted him, no matter what. It wasn't that way for everyone, and for whatever reason, Rick didn't want to tell his brothers. Brent had to respect the man's decision.

"Fuck, that feels good, Counselor, but I want more." Rick slid his hands into Brent's hair then tugged his head back. "Stand the fuck up."

Brent braced a hand on the seat of a nearby chair and leveraged himself to his feet. His jaw ached like a son of a bitch. He wiped drool from his chin with the flat of his hand then lifted his gaze to Rick's. The man's eyes were that of a wild animal trained on its next meal.

I'm his next meal.

The thought made every hair on Brent's body stand on end. He could run. Could tell him no and walk away, but Rick would hunt him down. Wear him down until he offered him his throat. The man standing before him, cannon of a cock in hand, wasn't the kind to back down once he'd decided something was his.

I want to be his.

His breath caught in his abused throat. He'd given himself to a lot of men but never in the way this one demanded with just a look. Rick's gaze commanded complete surrender. "Everything," it said.

Others had wanted his body. Wanted his ass. His cock. His mouth. None, not even Kenn, had wanted his heart, his soul. Did Rick know what he wordlessly asked? And would he give half as much in return? Or was this a one-way street?

The man blinked. Brent gasped as he glimpsed something hidden deep within. A pain buried beneath layers of hurt where it silently bled. A pain Rick lived with day in and day out.

Everything. It all made sense now. Rick had given everything and gotten nothing in return, so now he demanded it all up front in exchange for the only part of himself he was willing to give—his body.

The realization was akin to someone driving an invisible knife into his heart. He'd found someone who wanted everything from him, but in an ironic twist of fate, Rick had nothing to give him but a moment's pleasure. A chuckle rose to his throat, a hoarse rumble part tears, part self-deprecating humor. He'd come to Willowbrook looking for everything and had found it in a man who had already given it away.

"Turn around. Shove your pants down and bend over the table."

You want everything? You've got it. Had it since you shoved me up against that hotel room wall.

With nothing left to lose, Brent did as the man said.

CHAPTER FOURTEEN

The old Formica tabletop was as cold as ice beneath Brent's bare chest. Pressing his cheek to the table, he fisted his hands on either side of his head. Behind him, Rick sheathed his cock in preparation for taking what he wanted. Brent had steeled himself to be taken hard, without mercy, so when Rick leaned over him and dragged the butter dish into his line of sight, his heart nearly beat out of his chest.

"Grease yourself up or I'll take you raw. Makes no difference to me."

Thump. Thump. Thump. Brent reached out and curled his fingers into the stick. He'd set the butter out before he'd mixed the pancake batter. It was still cold as fuck but began to soften immediately as he touched it to blazing skin.

"Work it in good."

Thump. Thump. Thump. Brent reached for more. Once he'd coated the outside the best he could, he pushed one butter-coated finger past the initial barrier then withdrew.

"That's enough."

Brent returned his hand to the table and clenched it into a tight fist. At the same moment, Rick scooped up the butter remaining in the dish. *Dear god.* He'd never look at a pat of butter again without hearing the squishing, squashing sounds of the soft condiment being spread over latex sheathing. Never. In. His. Life. The sounds were erotic as hell in a disgustingly fascinating way. His heartbeat sped well past any measure of good health straight into heart-attack zone. Clearly, this man had experience in using whatever lubricant was handy. *What would he have used if the butter hadn't been on the table?*

Rick gripped his ass cheeks and spread him wide. When he notched the head of his cock at Brent's greased hole then slowly pressed forward, all thoughts, save one, left his mind. *I want everything, but I'll take anything.*

Oblivious to the butter on his hand, Brent pressed his forehead against the table, buried both hands in his hair, and tugged his scalp as hard as he could to distract himself from the overwhelming, the *insistent*, pressure against his asshole. Rick advanced like the Marine he was, breaching Brent's tight barrier like a battering ram. Once inside, he paused.

His voice as ragged as Brent's breathing, he whispered, "Fuck, you're tight."

Then he pushed forward in an uninterrupted march that expelled the breath from Brent's lungs and left him weak and limp. A prisoner of a war where he had no weapons. A war he didn't know how to fight.

His head swam from lack of oxygen, causing his involuntary muscles to awaken. He sucked in a breath then let it out on a groan. He was in quicksand and sinking fast. Grasping for purchase, he stretched his arms out and curled his fingers over the opposite edge of the table. His dick, harder than cast iron, hung against the front edge, throbbing with every heartbeat, aching for relief. His asshole was a ring of fire, made worse by the salt in the butter. Why the fuck hadn't he thought about that before? But god, he'd do it all over again to experience the feel, the fullness, the absolute rightness of Rick Ingram buried up inside him.

Two giant, work-worn hands splatted on the table next to his face as Rick curved his rock-hard body over Brent's boneless form. "That's right, Counselor. Hold on tight because I'm going to ride you so hard, you won't be able to walk." To emphasize his point, he withdrew almost all the way then tunneled back in. The table shook. Brent trembled. "When I'm through with you, I'm going to flip you over and suck you dry."

Then Rick made good on his promise, riding him hard. His balls slapping against Brent's, his carved hip bones digging into Brent's ass, his turgid shaft owning, claiming, with every forward thrust. Nothing had ever felt as good or hurt as bad. He loved that he could give Rick what he needed, but it hurt knowing the man had only this to give. All the while, tears rolled down Brent's cheeks as he told himself the biggest lie ever. *If this is all I ever have, it will be enough.*

His pajama pants had worked their way down to his ankles at some point. Rick's big hand slid the length of Brent's thigh then gripping him hard, lifted his knee to the table, opening him wider. The shift in position allowed Rick to go deeper. Every thrust came harder and deeper until Brent was sure it was Rick's cock shoving his heart into his throat. On the deepest, hardest thrust yet, Rick stopped and let his full weight rest on Brent's back. He nuzzled his ear, his hot breath causing Brent to break out in goose bumps all over. "You like that, Counselor? You like having my pole up your ass?"

"Yes. God, yes." The words came out on a whimper.

"You're so fucking hot and tight. I can feel your balls next to mine. You need to come, don't you?"

"Yes. Please."

"No." He nipped the shell of Brent's ear. "Do. Not. Fucking. Come. Not even when you feel me coming. Do you hear me?"

"Yes."

"If you disobey me, I'll *never* fuck you again. Never." He withdrew partway then barreled back in so hard, his balls slammed Brent's package up against the edge of the table. He cried out but refused to beg for mercy. "Is that what you want?"

"No." *God, no.*

"Good, because I want this ass every day." The words, spoken low and directly into his ear lit him up like a bolt of lightning, sparking every nerve ending in his body. Exhilaration coupled with fear made him tremble. Then Rick pushed himself upright. "I love seeing you this way." A big hand stroked along his spine. Brent groaned. "That's it. Purr for me. It feels so good on my cock." Brent groaned then rocked his hips up against Rick's crotch, silently begging him to move. Much more dirty talk, and he wouldn't be able to stop the orgasm building like a forest fire in his lower back.

Rick stroked Brent from shoulder to ass cheeks, pausing to finger his stretched hole. "Clench for me, baby."

He'd lost all control of his muscles long ago, so it took a few moments to focus on the ones in question and will them to obey Rick's command. A guttural curse, followed by, "Again," was as electrifying as sticking his dick in a light socket. Rick might be calling the shots, but Brent wasn't as helpless as he'd thought. He bore down on Rick's cock, squeezing it as tight as he could. The effort earned a whack to his right butt cheek and a strangled, "Fuck, that's good." So he clenched and released. Over and over. Other than to deliver sharp slaps to Brent's ass, Rick remained perfectly still while Brent massaged his cock. Rick might believe he had nothing left to give, but this one concession wrapped itself around Brent's heart and gave him hope where there had been none before.

"Enough!" Rick withdrew then rammed back in so, hard Brent saw stars. "You're a goddamn tease." The next thrust slapped Brent's dick against the edge of the table. Pain sliced through him, causing his legs to go numb and his knees to buckle. A silent cry fell from his open lips. The thrusts came faster and harder until blinding pain morphed into a need that cut him to the core. He was going to come. No way could he stop it. Then Rick fell atop him, hissed in his ear. "Don't do it. Don't you fuckin' come until you're in my mouth."

Rick leveraged himself up with a hand to the center of Brent's spine. A primal grunt rent the air. The cock impaling him thickened then throbbed inside him. Rick rocked into him, helpless in the face of his release. Brent had never experienced anything as intense as this. He was so fucking hard and on edge himself, but his own pleasure would be nothing in comparison to being on the receiving end of Rick's orgasm. He was going to be sore, but fuck, a little discomfort was a small price to pay for the privilege of experiencing Rick's total surrender to his own pleasure. The man who had let him go, and Brent was certain there was one, was an idiot.

Time seemed to stand still. Brent dragged in a shuddering breath and fought the tears threatening to spill over. The pressure eased as Rick lifted his restraining hand. Brent was trying to muster the energy to move when the two big paws returned, only this time, Rick stroked his back like he had before. Brent sighed and relaxed under the sensual touch. It was one thing to be this exposed in the throes of passion, but, in the aftermath, his skin might as well have been made of glass, brittle and transparent. He was certain Rick could see every emotion written on the walls of his wildly beating heart. A heart he could shatter so easily.

When he spoke, Rick's voice was as thick as the syrup in the container, now teetering on the edge of the table. "I love seeing my dick buried up inside your tight ass."

A hot finger rimmed his stretched hole. Brent squeezed his eyes shut to block the image his words evoked and willed his body not to respond to the intimate touch. He failed on both fronts.

"You like that?" The finger returned, traced the thinned line of sensitive muscle. Brent groaned, clenching his inner muscles around Rick's length. "Keep that up and I'll have another go at you."

Holy moly. "Is that a threat or a promise?" he croaked out.

"What do you want it to be?"

Brent licked his lips and swallowed hard. The answer came out on a whisper. "A promise."

Rick spread his cheeks wide. Brent groaned at the man's obvious perusal of his ass. "I wish I could see what you see."

"It's pretty spectacular," Rick admitted. He held Brent open with one hand while the other returned to a spot between his shoulder blades and pressed him hard against the Formica tabletop.

The man had just erupted like a volcano, yet he remained impossibly hard. Brent had no doubt he could go again, but he wasn't sure his ass was up for it. Rick was bigger than anyone he'd had before. Stronger, too. The way Rick overpowered him took his breath away—in a good way. "Now you're fishing for compliments."

"I was referring to your ass. I could stay here all day. But if I'm going to keep my promise to you and have another go at it, I'm going to have to give it a rest."

Brent's heart rose to his throat at the thought of Rick taking him again.

"I like seeing you this way. Taken. I like seeing my handprints on your skin." Using both hands, he squished Brent's cheeks together then slowly withdrew his cock, leaving Brent aching and emptier than he'd ever been in his life.

Rick covered Brent's hand with his. "Come on. Let me help you up." Brent took his hand and stood, turning so they were eye to eye. "Can you sit?" He indicated one of the kitchen chairs. "Or would you like the bed?"

Still in a brain fog from the thorough fucking coupled with an erection that might need medical attention, Brent replied, "Huh?"

Rick smiled then raised a hand to Brent's face. He tenderly stroked his jaw. Ran a thumb over his dry bottom lip. "I'm going to suck you dry. Remember?"

Later, Brent would wonder if that was the moment he fell in love with Rick Ingram or if it was later when he dropped to his knees between Brent's trembling thighs and made good on his promise.

Brent considered the state of his ass and the choices before him. "Bed," he whispered.

Rick reclaimed his hand and led him to his childhood bedroom, commanded him to sit on the edge of the bed then sank to his knees between Brent's trembling thighs. Rick wrapped one work-worn hand around the base of Brent's dick then bowed over the engorged head. His mouth was Heaven *and* Hell. Blazing hot yet soft and wet. Then he sucked Brent to the back of his throat, and he glimpsed the Pearly Gates.

"I…I can't…" He cradled Rick's head between his hands like a vise. His balls were the devil's hot coals as they drew up so far, they singed his vocal cords. He came on a ragged cry, hot cum searing his cock from the inside out as he spewed buckets of cum down Rick's throat.

Spent and fighting for breath, he released his hold on Rick's head and flopped back on the mattress. Rick licked and swallowed until Brent pleaded with him to stop. Between his ass and his cock, he didn't know which one was more tender. He'd be lucky if his balls descended anytime soon.

Rick hauled Brent fully onto the bed then flopped down beside him. Every muscle in his body ached, his heart most of all. Naked, he pretended to stare at the ceiling while he checked out Rick in his peripheral vision. Still wearing his pancake batter-splattered shirt, his flaccid cock resting in the V of his open jeans, an arm slung over his eyes, Rick looked like he was surrounded by land mines that could go off at the slightest movement.

Brent sighed and waded into the minefield. "I feel like I should say thank you."

"For?" The man's lips barely moved.

"You know. Everything. And I'm eternally grateful you're the kind of man who keeps his promises."

His admission earned him a grunt.

Okay. Sex talk was off the table. Pardon the pun. He searched the ceiling for another topic of conversation. "So…what was it like sharing this tiny room with two brothers?"

A muscle ticked in Rick's jaw. "Hell."

"I can imagine."

Rick tucked himself in and zipped up, leaving the top button of his jeans undone. He sat up then scooted to the edge of the bed. "No, you can't imagine." He ran a hand over his face. His shoulders slumped, but the earlier tension was still there, beneath the surface.

Brent sat up, placed a hand on Rick's shoulder. "Tell me."

"I don't want to talk about it."

Well, okay. "I thought you and your brothers were close." Brent slid to the floor in front of a suitcase that doubled as a makeshift dresser drawer and searched for another pair of pajama bottoms. He found a pair of sweatpants instead and pulled them on. "Jake talks about you and Will all the time."

Rick's eyebrows rose as if Jake mentioning his brothers was news to him. "We were close when we were kids. Had to be to survive."

The admission put every cell in Brent's body on alert. "Survive? What the hell are you talking about?"

Rick sighed and shook his head. "You aren't going to let this go, are you?"

Brent forced a smirk to his lips. "I'm a lawyer. What do you think?"

He patted the bed beside him. Brent sat, hands clasped in his lap. "Just remember, you asked."

"Really, Rick. You don't have to tell me if you don't want to."

"It's not like everyone in town didn't suspect. If you stay here long enough, you're bound to hear about the Brothers Grim."

"Brothers Grimm. As in the fairy tales?"

"Brothers grim, as in ghastly, gloomy, and glum. People don't think we know what they call us, but we've known since we were kids."

Wow, talk about a land mine. Brent had stepped on a doozy. In an effort to defuse the situation, he tried to inject a bit of humor. "Is that a collective description? If not, which one are you? I'd go with glum."

"Glum? Why not ghastly?"

"Honestly, none of you qualify as ghastly. Have you looked in a mirror? Jesus. The Ingram brothers won the genetic lottery for good looks. I could see Will as gloomy. Sometimes, he has that brooding artist look going on. So, that leaves glum, though I don't see it. People in this town must be crazy."

"I think the description is collective. As a unit, it probably fits."

"Explain."

CHAPTER FIFTEEN

Rick heaved a massive sigh as his gaze swept his childhood bedroom, letting the nightmares flood in. "We had bunk beds on this side of the room. Jake had his own twin bed on the other. Since I was the youngest, I had the lower bunk. I guess we had a pretty good life, even if we had to share a room. But then our mom died, and everything went to shit. Dad became a functioning alcoholic. To everyone outside our house, he was an upstanding citizen. A bastard but an upstanding citizen. Inside these walls, he was a tyrant. We all had chores, responsibilities. Jake had the most, then Will, then me. We had each other's backs, but there were times when it was impossible for us to get everything done, or if we did it get it done, it wasn't to his exacting standards. Thinking back, I'm convinced he set the bar high deliberately so he could punish us when we failed."

"No. Surely not."

Rick shrugged. Brent wrapped an arm around his waist and snuggled close. Odd, how the same body that aroused him like no other could also be comforting.

"Anyway, when we *failed*, he'd come looking for us. Jake took most of it. He'd stand between Dad and me and Will. I'd climb up, and Will and I would huddle in the corner of his bunk, as physically far away from him as we could get, but every blow Jake took hurt us, too. Afterward, he'd lay on his bed and say nothing. Will and I would go to sleep, eventually, but many nights we'd lay awake listening to Jake crying from the pain."

Rick stood, paced away, one hand on the back of his neck. "When Jake left for college, Will and I became the primary targets of Dad's rage. Will did his best to protect me, but there wasn't anywhere for either of us to hide. We spent as much time out of the house as possible, but we eventually had to come home.

Will had always been into art. Drawing and painting. That wasn't a macho enough career choice in Dad's eyes, so he beat Will, even when he was little, for being, in his words, a sissy. He left for New York the day after his high school graduation. I hated Jake for the longest, for leaving us, then I hated Will for leaving. I still had my diploma in my hand when I showed up at the Marine recruiting office. I couldn't get out of here fast enough.

"I didn't know what I was getting myself into. Looking back, I think I was trying to impress Dad. I knew I was gay. Had known since I hit puberty, and I was more fascinated with cock than pussy. If the Marines weren't macho enough for Dad, what was? Because, if Will's career choice disappointed him, god help me if he found out I was gay." He leaned against the far wall, crossed his arms over his chest in an effort to hide his shaking hands. Though his brothers had asked him to explain many times, he'd never told anyone why he'd enlisted. He didn't know why he was telling his brother's lackey now. "A lot of guys washed out in boot camp but not me. There wasn't anything my drill sergeant could do to me that was worse than what my own father had done or what he would do if I failed. So, I stuck. I was still hiding who I was, but I'd learned to fight back. The guys in my unit became my brothers, and, like my flesh-and-blood brothers, they'd risk their life to save mine. The feeling was mutual, but it was a lonely existence—until I met Dave."

Rick studied the toes of his boots. Brent jumped to his feet, took Rick's hand in his, and led him out of the room. "Come on. You can talk while I clean up the mess we made in the kitchen."

"Yeah. Let me change my shirt." Rick disengaged his hand from Brent's. "Then I'll help you clean up."

At Brent's nod, Rick hurried to his room, closed the door, and leaned against it. What the fuck was he doing? He'd broken every rule he'd ever made for himself. He'd screwed a man he had no business wanting, much less touching. Then he'd talked about his childhood and why he'd enlisted. He shook his head. *Fuck.* He was losing his mind. He'd never told Dave about his childhood. Had never told him why he'd joined the Marines. And Dave had never asked. Grabbing fists full of hair, he doubled over, his stomach cramping as the truth hit him. Their relationship had always been about Dave. Every conversation. His Marine fuck buddy hadn't given two shits about Rick's life. All he'd cared about was fucking. Rick sucked in a breath. *He never loved me. And I never loved him.*

Not the way I...

Ah, fuck. He slid down the door till his ass hit the floor. *I'm not in love with Brent.*

Not yet.

Knock. Knock. "You okay in there?"

Shit. Rick scrambled to his feet, yanked off his soiled shirt. "Yeah. Sorry. Just answering a text from Jake." *Liar.* He pulled a clean T-shirt from a drawer and yanked it over his head. "I'll be right there." For good measure, he shot off a preemptive text to Will and Jake letting them know he was fine and inquiring about the snow level at Jake's place out by the lake. He was thumbing a reply to the barrage of text replies when he entered the kitchen a few minutes later.

"There you are." Brent, once again wearing his ridiculous apron, stood at the sink, a soapy sponge in one hand and plate in the other. The scene smacked of domesticity, and fuck, if that wasn't a turn-on. When he turned around, unshed tears shimmered in the man's eyes. "I'm sorry. Didn't mean to rush you. I just thought…"

Rick closed the distance between them, took the bowl and sponge out of the man's hands, and set them in the sink. Then he pulled him in for a hug. No one except his brothers had worried about him the way this man did after only knowing him for a few short weeks. "Shh." He rubbed his hands over the man's bare back in what he hoped was a soothing manner. Brent wound his arms around Rick's waist and tucked his cheek against his chest. Fuck, it felt good to hold him. "I'm fine," he whispered, placing a kiss on the top of his head. "Thanks for coming to check on me."

Brent dug his fingers into Rick's back. "After our talk. I mean, I know it hurt to talk about all that stuff, but I'm glad you told me."

Rick slid the tips of his fingers beneath the waistband of Brent's sweatpants and slowly stroked the skin there. Brent stiffened in his arms. "I need to touch you," he said, dipping his hand lower to cover his cheek. "Are you okay with that?"

"Yeah." His breath hitched. "Totally."

Between them, Rick's erection throbbed to life. With his hand on Brent's ass, he nudged him forward until they were pelvis to pelvis, their boners trapped between them. The man had an impressive cock. It was about the same length as Rick's with enough girth a guy would know he was being fucked. He wasn't ready to go there yet. Wasn't sure he ever would be. Whatever this was with Brent was temporary. Had to be. The longer they lived under the same roof, the more likely someone would find out they'd become fuck buddies. The thought of coming out to his brothers sent a tremor down his spine.

Brent placed a kiss on Rick's neck. "I know how you feel. I'm sore as fuck, but I want you again."

"Jesus!" Rick cupped the man's ass, his fingers searching out the source of Brent's discomfort. "We shouldn't." He dipped his middle finger between his cheeks to stroke the tight pucker.

Brent clenched around his finger. His hot breath fanned the erratic pulse in Rick's neck. "God, that feels good. Inside. Please?"

"Are you sure?"

"Put your fucking finger in me. Now, please."

Rick stifled the laugh rising in his throat. God, Brent was going to be the death of him. He withdrew his hand and stepped back. If he was going to do this, he was going to do it right. No more kitchen table sex. "My room. Take that hideous apron off and lay on the bed."

"Are you always this bossy?"

He hadn't been with Dave, had followed the man's orders in and out of bed. But this was different. Brent was different. He made Rick want things he'd never wanted before. Having this man do his bidding pushed his horny button. "Yes. Do you have a problem with that?"

Brent shook his head. "No. I was just wondering."

"Now you know."

"Yes, I do."

Rick caught the smile on Brent's face as he hurried from the room. Feet braced shoulder width apart, his hands bracketed behind his head, he silently counted to ten before he followed.

~ ~ ~

Rick hadn't specifically said to get naked, but Brent went the extra mile, shucking his sweats along with the apron the second he crossed the threshold into Rick's bedroom. Seeing how neat the room was, bed made, no clothes on the floor, he carefully folded his garments and placed them on the dresser before crawling to the center of the king-sized bed. When Rick appeared in the doorway, Brent was ready for him, one hand behind his neck, the other stroking his cock.

Fuck, the man was gorgeous. The waffle-knit Henley clung to his muscular torso and arms, and lord, jeans like his should be illegal. Eyeing the bulge at his crotch, Brent's mouth watered, and his ass involuntarily clenched at the memory of how well Rick filled him. Yeah, he was sore, and he should have taken the time to clean the salted butter off, but he sort of liked how the slight sting and greasy feel reminded him how it felt to be impaled by Rick's enormous cock. He didn't know what the man had in mind, but he hoped it involved stretching his ass some more.

"Nice." Rick grabbed the hem of his shirt and yanked it over his head. He took the time to fold it then placed it next to Brent's clothes on the dresser. Then he released the button on his jeans and slowly pulled the zipper down.

Brent couldn't take his eyes off the strip of pale skin revealed as the garment parted one slow inch at a time. There was something sexy as fuck about a guy who went commando. Especially in a pair of tight jeans. He licked his lips in anticipation of a glimpse of the man's erection then groaned as he saw it was tucked to one side, safely out of reach of the zipper's teeth. Hell's bells. The man knew how to do a striptease. Strangling his dick to keep from coming, he gritted out, "And you call me a tease."

"You are a tease, and a fucking temptation." Rick kicked his shoes off then hooked his thumbs in the waistband of his jeans. "Did I tell you to take your pants off?"

"No." His confidence slipped a notch. "I assumed…"

"Lucky for you, you assumed right. This time." Rick shoved his jeans past his hips. His impressive erection sprang free. The pearl of precum decorating the tip bolstered Brent's confidence straight to the stratosphere. He hadn't read the situation wrong. This proud, broken warrior wanted him. "Knees up. Spread your legs."

Brent complied. Rick strolled to the end of the bed, affording him an unobstructed view. Brent's thighs trembled under his heated gaze.

"Raise your legs up. Let me see your hole."

Hooking his hands beneath his thighs, he brought his knees up to his shoulders, exposing himself fully. He'd swear hours had passed before the end of the bed dipped under Rick's weight and set Brent's entire body vibrating.

"Stay like that. Let me look at you."

Brent whimpered and called upon the universe to give him strength. His lungs strained, air shuddering in only to be trapped there until being expelled all at once. Rick's gaze raked over him, from his eyes to his leaking cock, to his throbbing balls, then settling on his thoroughly used asshole. The longer Rick stared, the more Brent shook with need for the man to touch him. When he did—a single blunt finger tracing a line of fire around, but not actually touching, his portal—Brent groaned, his butthole clenching in blatant invitation.

"God, that's beautiful." Then his finger was there, pushing, gentle but insistent.

Tears streamed down his temples as he pressed eagerly against the single digit. "I need you."

The words were barely out of his mouth before Rick leaned over him. Braced on one arm, he thumbed Brent's tears with his free hand. "Shh, baby. You're too sore." He made a sound of protest Rick stole from his lips with a kiss so achingly sweet, it cracked something open in his heart. "I'm still going to take care of you." His big hand gently swept hair off Brent's forehead. "Do you *want me* to take care of you?"

Fresh tears blurred his vision, and his arms shook with the need to embrace this incredible man with the heart of gold. He'd been through more than any child should have to endure and came out on the other side a protector. *More than you can know, Marine. More than you can ever know.* "Yes. Please. Please, Rick."

Holding Brent's gaze, Rick snaked his free hand between them. He palmed his erection and balls then slid lower until his middle finger probed the tender ring of muscles. "Relax. Let me in."

Brent emptied his lungs. At the same time, Rick breached his opening, burying his thick finger deep inside him. Brent tensed at the sudden sting. *Ring of fire.* The saying had new meaning. He sucked in a deep breath as his body adjusted and the burn eased.

"Told you you were too sore for my dick."

Nodding, Brent concentrated on breathing. In. Out. "Doesn't make me want you any less."

"Don't say shit like that or I'll forget my manners."

God save me from protective men. "I don't want your manners. I want your cock."

"Put your legs down and take both our cocks in your hand, then."

Brent lowered his shaking legs. His feet hit the mattress then he reached between them and wrapped his hand around both cocks.

Rick sucked in a harsh breath, bowing his head so their foreheads touched. "Fuck, that feels good." Brent tightened his hold, stroking upward then back down. "Do that again." He repeated the move, faster this time. Rick bucked his hips, driving his cock hard against Brent's. "Hold on tight, baby. I'm going to fuck your hand and your ass at the same time." He flexed his hips and his hand at the same time, drilling his finger deep into Brent's ass while his cock thrust hard.

Brent threw his head back and, clamping his jaw tight, lost himself to Rick's ministrations.

"That's it, baby. Lay there and let me make you feel good." Rick placed a kiss on Brent's upturned chin then trailed a line of open-mouth kisses down the slope of his throat.

"So…so good."

"I love the way you taste. I love how tight your ass is. I love your hard cock rubbing against mine." He added a second finger, stretching him wide. The delicious fullness overrode the sting.

I love...you. Brent groaned as the unexpected thought blossomed in his head then spread like an electrical charge throughout his body, lighting up every nerve ending, leaving him teetering on the edge.

"I need you to come, baby." Rick's voice sounded like he'd gargled glass shards. His cock swelled in Brent's grip, signaling his impending release.

"Please," Brent pleaded on a whisper.

"Love. This. Ass." He punctuated each of the first two words with a hard thrust then, on the last one, he added a third digit and buried his fingers so deep, Brent swore the man tapped his heart.

He came, Rick's name stolen from his lips by the man who'd stolen his heart.

CHAPTER SIXTEEN

"Good morning." Brent halted in the doorway. He'd tamed his bedhead hair and shaved the scruff he'd let grow over the weekend. Dressed for work in a navy-blue suit, white shirt, and red tie, he looked like he'd just walked off the cover of GQ. Rick's dick instantly became nuclear hard.

Leaning against the counter, his first cup of coffee in hand, he motioned to the range. "I put water on for your tea."

Brent drank coffee but preferred tea. Just one of the things Rick had learned about the man over the last few days. He'd also discovered his roommate had an insatiable appetite for sex which Rick had taken full advantage of. His ass had to be sore today after all the times they'd fucked. Rick's dick twitched, reminding him he was a little chafed himself. They'd had "the discussion" and thankfully, dispensed with condoms late Saturday afternoon when it became apparent they would soon run out. It was either have the talk or quit fucking. They'd had the talk.

"Thanks." Brent took a mug from the cabinet then selected a tea bag from the box of assorted flavors he'd purchased Friday afternoon before the snowstorm hit. "I guess it's back to work today. At least for me. What about you?"

"As much as I'd like to take you back to bed and keep you there another day, I've got work to do." Rick nodded at the window above the sink. "Roads are mostly clear. If you drive anywhere, be careful. There could still be black ice in places."

"I was going to walk to work, but I think I'll take my car. I took a look out front and the sidewalk's a mess."

Rick's gaze dropped to the floor. "Yeah, the slush and salt would probably ruin those fancy shoes."

Brent shuffled closer so the two men were almost toe-to-toe. "Don't mock my fancy shoes, Marine."

Rick laughed at the man's feigned outrage. "You and your fancy suits." He fingered Brent's silk tie, let it slip through his grasp. "So put together. So fucking uptight. You need to loosen up a bit." He slid his hand down, palmed the hard ridge in his slacks. Brent's groan spurred him on. They'd had good reasons for skipping morning sex, but those reasons weren't sounding so good now. "I should take care of this for you."

Brent shifted his hips away. "We shouldn't."

Rick slipped his fingers beneath Brent's waistband and tugged him closer. He searched the man's face for real resistance and found only need in his eyes. "Maybe not," he conceded, "but it won't take long." He nuzzled the spot beneath his ear he knew made Brent's knees weak. "God, you smell good. Let me have a taste. I'll be quick, I promise."

Brent tilted his head, allowing Rick better access. He took advantage, placing soft kisses on his neck, along his jaw, then up to his lips where he teased the corner with his tongue. He pushed his hand lower, skimming his erection with his fingertips. "Let me fix your little problem."

"Little?" His breathing erratic, his protest was half-hearted at best.

Knowing he would win the round, Rick chuckled. "Then you're admitting you have a big problem and it needs to be addressed."

"Fuck you." Brent pushed him away then fumbled with his zipper. In seconds, he had his shaft out, pumping it with his fist. "This is all your fault, so fix it, asshole."

Rick dropped to his knees. Brushing Brent's hand away, he took over, his grip tight around the velvet-covered steel. "All you had to do was ask," he said, eyeing the magnificent cock in his hand. "You know I'll take care of you."

"Just fucking get on with it. I've got to get to the office."

He'd promised to be quick, but he'd lied. He didn't give a rat's ass if Brent was late for work. With a flick of his tongue, he captured a bead of precum dripping from his slit.

"Fuuuck," Brent cried. "Get on with it. I'm dying here."

Rick smiled then laved the bulbous head with his tongue. Brent hissed and flexed his hips, shoving his dick at Rick's face. The man was too easy to tease. Rick sat back on his heels, his gaze sweeping Brent from head to toe. "I love this look on you. Sexy-as-fuck lawyer, all buttoned-up with your dick hanging out like the horny bitch you are."

Gripping the counter like his life depended on it, Brent responded, "You know what I like better than seeing you on your knees, Marine?"

Rick captured the dick bobbing in front of him and licked the tip. "What's that, Counselor?"

"You, on your knees, sucking my dick." He grabbed Rick's head in both hands. "Open the fuck up and let me in."

Rick obliged, taking Brent to the back of his throat. Then he closed his lips around his girth and sucked.

"Holy fuckin' mother of god, that feels good." Brent grabbed for the countertop as Rick licked and sucked and pumped, driving him to the brink then easing off only to do it all over again. He tasted too good, and the sexy-as-fuck sounds he made were the best kind of aphrodisiac. Rick could suck him off all day long and never grow tired of it. The tea kettle sent up an unholy howl they both ignored.

Then it stopped.

"Good morning, bro," an all-too-familiar voice called.

"Holy shit!" Brent withdrew fast like he'd accidentally stuck his dick in a pencil sharpener. He tucked his withering erection back in his pants, yanking the zipper up lightning fast. With an apologetic glance at Rick, he hurried out of the room.

Rick, eyes closed as his world came crashing down around his ears, blew out a pent-up breath. Refusing to meet his brother's gaze, he slowly regained his feet. He wiped his mouth on his sleeve then placed his coffee mug in the microwave, staring at it as it spun around inside. Behind him, Will popped a pod in the brewer for his own cup of coffee.

Shit. He should have known his nosy-ass brother wouldn't leave until he had an explanation. Like what he'd walked in on needed explaining. Will might be a busybody, all up in his business, but he wasn't stupid. He knew exactly what he'd walked in on.

Nuking the coffee bought him a few seconds to get his shit together. Not nearly enough time, but it was all he was going to get. Mug in hand, he dropped into a chair and took a sip of the steaming liquid, swallowing past the steel band tightening around his chest. He didn't want to have this conversation with Will, or anyone else, for that matter. In all the times he'd imagined coming out to his family, he'd never imagined it happening like this. "I thought I told you to knock."

"I did. You couldn't hear me"—he motioned toward the kettle he'd removed from the burner—"probably because of Mom's old kettle. Thing sounds like a banshee. So, I let myself in." He retrieved his filled cup from the brewer, rummaged in the fridge for milk then added some to his drink before joining Rick at the table, as if he hadn't just turned his life upside down and inside out.

Silence settled between them. When the swish and thud of the front door opening then closing met his ears, Rick raised his gaze to Will's. "It's none of your business."

His brother sipped then carefully set his mug on the table. "I know it isn't, but I still want to know why you hid this from us."

"What makes you think I've been hiding something? Maybe this was a one-time thing."

"Don't bullshit me, baby brother. Unlike you, I didn't fall off a turnip truck."

"Fuck you." Rick jerked to his feet, giving his brother his back.

"Whoa. Hold it right there. First, that would be incest, and second, I don't swing that way."

Rick groaned. "Can you at least try to be serious here?" He stomped to the sink, braced his hands on either side, and stared out the window at the bleak winter landscape. "This is my life we're talking about."

"You're right, bro. It's your life, and as you pointed out, your sexual orientation isn't any of my business. But *you* are my business."

Water dripped from the eaves like a cold heartbeat. "How do you figure that?"

"You're my brother. I've got your back, always. No matter what." He paused to sip his drink. "Let me ask you something. Does it matter to you that *I'm* not gay?"

He shook his head. "No."

"Then why the fuck would it matter to me if *you* are?"

Rick shrugged, letting Will's question sink in. Could it be that simple? Would his brothers accept his being gay so easily? Taking a deep breath and letting it out, he blinked away the tears threatening to fall and faced his brother. "You really don't care?"

"Fuck, no, I don't care."

"I used to wonder if you were gay."

"Me? Why the fuck would you think that? Oh! Because I'm an artist?" Will laughed. "Stereotyping much, baby brother?"

Relieved the conversation hadn't gone the way he'd feared, Rick smiled. "Maybe."

"And I never suspected you were. Probably because you joined the Marines. The biggest, baddest motherfuckers on the planet. How did that work out for you?"

Rick turned back to the window. "I got fucked."

CHAPTER SEVENTEEN

"Want to explain?"

Rick shook his head. "Look, Will. I don't want to talk about any of this, and I especially don't want to talk about my time in the Corps. Why don't you tell me why you came by, and let's forget this ever happened?"

"You've been fucked up since you came home. I know I wasn't here when your enlistment was up, but I am now. Jake and I thought you were in for the long haul. You were a Marine for eight fucking years."

"I'm still a Marine."

"I get it, *Semper fi*, and all that shit, but Jake and I both knew something happened or you would have re-upped. Did someone give you shit because you're gay? Is that it?"

God, both his brothers could be a pain in the ass, but Will, especially, was like a dog with a bone. He didn't know when to let something go. "Forget it, Will. I don't want to talk about the Corps."

"Fine." Will raised his hands in surrender. "Then let's talk about your roommate."

Hands clenched into fists; Rick spun around. "I don't want to talk about him, either. Leave it alone."

"Why?" His brother stood. "Why won't you talk about him?"

"Because he's none of your fucking business. It was a one-time thing. Over."

"Who are you trying to convince? Me? Or yourself?" Will poured the rest of his coffee in the sink, rinsed the cup, and placed it in the dishwasher. "You've been living a lie long enough, don't you think? No one who loves you will give a shit about your sexual orientation."

Rick huffed out a breath. "That's a short list in this town, brother."

"The rest of them don't matter…brother." He paused in the doorway. "For what it's worth, I'm sorry I interrupted." A smile broke across his face. "It looked like both of you were enjoying the blow job. *Oorah!* brother."

Rick listened for the front door to shut before collapsing to the floor, his back to the range, his knees drawn up. "Shit."

He raked a hand through his hair, his heart pounding like a racehorse out of the starting gate. Will hadn't said so, but he would tell Jake. They'd both tell their women. He kicked out at the nearest chair leg, slamming the chair against a nearby cabinet. His days in the closet were over. Give it twenty-four hours, forty-eight tops, and everyone in Willowbrook would know. "Fuck!"

So much for his fledgling business. Who the hell in this town would hire him now? He squeezed his eyes shut as reality sliced him in half. The fuck of it was, they *had* been enjoying the blow job, and no matter how much he wished Will hadn't walked in on them, he couldn't wish the interlude away, and he hoped to fuck Brent felt the same way. But after that scene? All bets were off.

Rising to his feet, he washed out his coffee mug and set it in the drainer to dry. If he worked through lunch and skipped dinner, he might be able to finish the job he was on today. Tomorrow, he'd start work on the apartment above Sunny's gallery downtown. The sooner he got that done, the sooner Brent would move out and talk would die down. In the meantime, he had no choice but to act like nothing had happened. He grabbed the lunch box he'd packed earlier, slamming the back door behind him on his way out.

He finished the last coat of paint on the Riverton's living room wall and sat down to eat his lunch when the doorbell rang. The homeowners were away on a Caribbean cruise while Rick worked on their house. He opened the door, sandwich in hand. "Well, shit." Shaking his head, he stood back, holding the door open so his oldest brother could step inside. "Wipe your damn feet. They had the hardwood floors refinished last week." Appetite lost, he tossed the sandwich in his soft-sided cooler then stood, arms crossed and feet braced apart. Jake shut the door behind him then wiped his feet on the old towel Rick had left by the door. "Fucking Will and his big mouth."

Jake fixed him with a glare. "Don't blame this on Will. I asked him to stop by your place this morning. It's not his fault you had a mouth full of dick at the time."

Heart pounding, jaw clenching, Rick flexed the fingers on both hands, prepared to beat the ever-loving shit out of his brother if he went down the homophobe road. "He should have fucking knocked."

Jake shrugged. "He said he did. That's neither here nor there. The fact remains, you've been lying to us." He raked a hand through his hair. "What the fuck, Rick? We're your family. Both of us stood up for you until you were big enough to stand up for yourself. You're a fucking Marine, for god's sake. I can't even imagine the shit you've seen and done, but you didn't have the guts to tell your flesh and blood that you're gay? I tell you, brother, that hurts." He placed a fist over his heart.

Rick blinked. "I didn't think it was any of your business."

"Fuck you." Jake crossed the room, got up in his face. "You. Are. My. Business. I went through hell to protect you and Will, and this is the way you repay me?"

"I didn't ask to be gay."

Jake snarled, grabbed the neck of Rick's shirt, and dragged him close so they were nose to nose. "Get this through your thick skull. I. Don't. Care if you like dick or not. But I do care that you didn't think you could confide in me." He released his hold, shoved Rick back a step. "Don't ever fucking keep things like that from me again. Do you hear me?"

Rick choked back tears. "Yeah. I hear you."

Jake paced away, rubbing the back of his neck. "How long have you known?"

Rick shrugged. "Since I was a kid. Puberty, I guess."

His brother spun around. "You wound me, brother."

"I wanted to tell you, but I hardly knew what it meant myself. You and Will dated. You talked about pussy and tits and"—he shrugged self-consciously—"I thought I'd eventually grow up enough to appreciate girls, but it never happened. I dated girls. You know I did. I kissed 'em and made out. Felt 'em up, but in the back of my mind, I was wishing I was pawing the quarterback instead of the cheerleader. My thoughts and desires went against everything I was taught to expect from my body—yet, there I was, having wet dreams about guys." Rick sank to the floor, his back to the wall. "Then there was Dad. He hated Will for being an artist. Can you imagine what he would have done if he'd found out I was gay?"

Jake sat on a capped five-gallon paint can. "You're absolutely right. Dad would have shit a brick."

"Or thrown one at me."

His brother nodded. "Yeah. I'm sorry, Rick. You shouldn't have had to go through that alone."

"It would have been nice to have someone to talk to, I suppose, but honestly, I'm not sure I would have said anything even if Dad had been the opposite of what he was. I was scared to act on my desires. Thought if I tried hard enough, I could be like everyone else, but it wasn't something I could change. It was just me."

"So, why the fuck did you enlist?"

Rick rubbed a hand over his face. "At the time, I just wanted to get the fuck out of this town, like you and Will. But in hindsight, I think I was trying to prove to myself that I wasn't gay and at the same time, make sure Dad never suspected."

"Fucking Marines," Jake muttered. "You took decades off my life. I worried about you every fucking day."

"I'm sorry. I was only in real danger a couple of times, and I had a lot of good men at my back."

"Will said when he asked you about the Marines you said you got fucked. What did you mean by that?"

"Will has a big fucking mouth."

"He loves you as much as I do. When you came home, you were, for lack of a better phrase, fucked up. Will and I came up with the idea of you renovating the house to get you out of your own head." He surveyed the newly painted room.

"Never thought you'd turn it into a business, but we're proud of you anyway."

"Let's just say, I left something behind, and I wasn't happy about it."

"Something or someone?"

"Both?" He stood. "The Corps was more than a job. It was a family. A brotherhood. I missed it when I came home, more than I thought I would."

Jake got to his feet. "I'm sorry you miss it, but I'm not sorry you're home." He crossed to the front door. "I asked Will to walk down and talk to you before you went to work this morning. I'd been trying to reach you, but your phone must have been off."

He'd been preoccupied with Brent and had completely forgotten about his phone. "I forgot to plug it in. I didn't notice it was dead until this morning." He cocked his head toward an outlet on the far end of the room. "I plugged it in as soon as I got here."

"I thought you were just ignoring me."

"Nah. I'd never do that." He cracked his first smile since he'd opened the door to find Jake on the porch. "So, what did you want?"

"We're having a little thing tonight. Wanted to do it Saturday, but the weather fucked up our plans."

"What kind of thing?"

"They call it a gender reveal. It's something new, I guess. At least, I'd never heard of it. Come. Have dinner with us. For dessert we've got a cake. It's either pink or blue inside. When we cut it, we'll know if we're having a girl or a boy."

"Why don't you just tell me now?"

"Because we don't know. Sunny's doctor put it in a sealed envelope. We took it straight to the bakery, so only the baker and her doctor know." He rolled his eyes. "Sounds stupid to me, but whatever my wife wants, she gets."

"And she wants to torture everyone she knows with a gender reveal party."

Jake pointed a finger at him. "You got it." He opened the door then turned back. "Six o'clock. Bring Brent."

CHAPTER EIGHTEEN

Brent ignored the call from his sister and yanked open the door to his place of employment. Jean, Jake's legal secretary, and by extension his, sat at her desk, a steaming cup of coffee resting on a coaster next to her keyboard. She was hard at work. On what, he didn't know or care.

With the hem of his pants damp and muddy, his shoes squeaking with every step, he stopped in front of her desk and tried for a pleasant smile but knew he failed miserably. "Good morning."

He hated to interrupt her workflow, but shit happened. Like being interrupted in the middle of a blow job by a family member. Jean would get over it. He wasn't so sure about Rick. Will's interruption had ruined Brent's day, and possibly his lover's life, and he felt guilty as hell about that. He should have refused Rick's advances this morning. They'd existed in a snow globe environment the last few days, but he'd known as soon as he saw the sun streaming through Rick's bedroom window this morning, their time was up. Boy, how right he'd been.

Jean smiled up at him. "Good…lord. What happened to you?" Her gaze raked his soiled suit and ruined shoes.

"I walked to work." He'd done it nearly every day since moving into Rick's house, but today, he should have gone back into the house when he'd realized he'd left without his keys, coat, or briefcase. Warmer temperatures had turned the snow to slush with icy patches underneath in places. More than once he'd narrowly escaped ending up on his ass. Then he'd been on the receiving end of a muddy shower, courtesy of a trash truck that had barreled through a puddle.

"Why in heaven's name would you walk on a day like today? Is there something wrong with your car?"

"Nah. I just wasn't thinking." Truth. His mind had been on Rick, and how he'd left him to face his brother alone. It was a chicken-shit thing to do but when he'd left the room, Rick hadn't called him back. Call him a coward, but he didn't want to get in the middle of whatever was going to transpire once he left. He'd been caught with his dick in his boss's brother's mouth by another of his boss's brothers.

"Well, there are some towels in the cabinet next to the sink in the bathroom. You should take your socks and shoes off and let them dry. You don't have any appointments this morning, but you have two this afternoon."

Brent nodded as she rambled on. When she ran out of sage advice, he said what had been on his mind when he stopped at her desk. "Can you take another look at the real estate market in town? See if something had come on the market recently? Sale or rental, I don't care. I'll take anything."

Jean's eyes narrowed, and her lips pursed. "Something wrong with where you're at?"

After this morning, Rick is going to toss me out on my ass. Brent lied through his teeth. "I'd really like to have my own place."

The woman's eyes softened, and her lips curved up on the corners. "Oh, I get it. Need your privacy?" She chuckled. "Grown man. Single. I get it." She winked and waved him away. "I'll see what I can do."

Christ on a cracker. He kicked his shoes off, picked them up then padded in his wet socks to his office and shut the door. Leaning against the closed portal, he sighed. What was it with middle-aged women and their need to see everyone paired off for a cruise on Noah's Ark? He hadn't told her he was gay, not because he was hiding it but because he didn't think it should matter to anyone but him. Thank god, Jean only had boys or she probably would have tried to fix him up the first week he was here.

He tossed his shoes behind his desk. Settling into his desk chair, he removed his socks and spread them out on the floor next to his shoes. At lunch he'd go back to the house, change clothes, and get the car and briefcase he'd left behind. He'd completely forgotten about the papers he'd taken home on Friday. After asking Jean to print another copy for him, he forced himself to concentrate on work instead of the man he'd inadvertently outed to his family in the worst possible way.

The morning passed slower than molasses in winter. As soon as Brent could reasonably consider taking a lunch break, he put his soggy socks and shoes back on and hurried to Rick's cozy bungalow for a change of clothes. He tossed his soiled suit in the bag he kept for his dry cleaning then donned clean slacks and a shirt.

He'd skipped breakfast in favor of other things and, after the interruption, never got around to eating. Stepping into the kitchen, he closed his eyes. The earlier scene, permanently embedded in his reel of all-time worst moments, played on a continuous loop. He could still see Rick leaning against the counter, coffee mug in hand, dressed in paint-splattered jeans, plaid shirt layered over a long-sleeved T-shirt, and work-worn boots. The scruff shading his jaw and sexy mussed hair had added to his barely tamed appearance. Despite being sore from the man's attentions the last few days, he'd wanted him more than he could recall ever wanting someone. The offer of a blow job had been too good to refuse. Breakfast was overrated anyway.

Shaking the memory loose, he crossed to the refrigerator. Coming up with a container of leftover pasta from Friday night, he popped it in the microwave. He'd no sooner settled in to eat than his phone dinged with an incoming message.

Rick: *Don't cook for me tonight. I'll be out late.*

Brent stared at the message, wondering if Rick needed to work late or if he was avoiding him because of what had happened earlier. If it was the latter, discussing it over text message wasn't a good idea, and if it was the former, he'd just have to accept that Rick had deadlines to meet and sometimes would miss supper. Either way, there wasn't anything he could do about it, so he replied with a thumbs-up emoji and resumed his meal.

Jean greeted him with a wide smile upon his return. He smiled back, because it was impossible not to, and stopped at her desk. "What's got you so happy? Did Bill Gates call and say he's fed up with his current slate of attorneys and wants to hire us?"

"Nope. I just got off the phone with Jake. He and Sunny are having a gender reveal tonight."

It was all he could do to keep a smile on his face. Rick wasn't working late. He was going to a party at his brother's house and didn't want Brent to know. *Maybe he didn't know if I was invited and was protecting my feelings.*

"I asked him if you knew how to get to his house and he said not to worry, that you were coming with Rick." As if she hadn't just shattered all his illusions, she prattled on, "I never thought I'd see the day Jake Ingram settled down, much less became a father, but here we are. I wonder what if it will be, a boy or a girl? What are the odds?"

"Fifty-fifty," he answered robotically. Did Jake know about what Will had walked in on this morning, or had he told Rick to bring his tenant along?

Jean giggled. Lord, he didn't know women her age still did that. The weirdness of it shook his feet loose from the floor. He purposely strode toward his office. Jean called out to him, "Your first appointment is in fifteen minutes. I'll give you a holler when they get here."

He raised his hand, signaling he'd heard her then shut his door and leaned against it. What the hell was he supposed to do now? If he didn't go, would his employer be offended? If he did go, would Rick be pissed? Yes, was the answer to both questions, so his decision came down to which Ingram brother he wanted to offend the least. One could fire him. The other could render him homeless.

The intercom buzzed, forcing him over to his desk. He pressed the button and the secretary's voice filled the room. "I have a call for you on line one. A Kenneth Westinghouse. He says it's important."

And the hits keep on comin'. He sat in his chair, dropped his elbows to the desk, and his head into his upturned palms. *I never should have gotten out of bed this morning.*

"Mr. Whitehall?"

"Brent? What should I tell him?"

Holding the button down, he replied, "Thanks, Jean. I'll take the call."

Heart pounding, he picked up the receiver and punched the blinking button indicating an incoming call. "Hey, Kenn."

"Brent. It's good to hear your voice."

At the sound of the deep voice he'd loved so much, his racing heart shifted into overdrive. "What's up?" It was a lame question considering this was a man he'd asked to make a life with him just a few short weeks ago.

There was a long silence then a heavy sigh came over the line. "I want you to come back. I'm miserable without you. We'll get a house in the burbs, if that's what you want. A picket fence. A dog. I talked to Everett at your old office. He said he'd take you back. They miss you, too."

Of all the things Kenn said, his brain stuck on the last one. "You called Everett?" Everett was another attorney at Brent's former firm, and he was flamboyantly gay.

"I saw him at a party, and we got to talking. You know how it is."

He knew exactly how it was. Kenn had always had a thing for Everett. They'd met socially on numerous occasions, and, oblivious to Brent's embarrassment, his former lover had flirted with Everett shamelessly.

"You slept with him, didn't you?" The silence on the other end was all the answer he needed. "Why did you call me, Kenn?" He now knew the call had nothing to do with wanting him back.

"I told you. I miss you. Everett misses you." More silence. The kind Brent didn't feel like filling, so he waited. "Ev has a place at the lake. It's a big house. Plenty of room for the three of us. Room to party. Entertain."

Ev? He was calling him Ev now? Jesus, the man had nerve. The nickname was a spear to his heart and proof he'd done the right thing when he'd left, even if he'd chosen the wrong place to go. Squaring his shoulders, he clenched the handset tight. "Let me get this straight. I asked you to move to Willowbrook with me, to make a life with me, and you declined. Then you have the audacity to call me up and tell me you're fucking one of my former coworkers and the two of you want me to move back, shack up with you out at the lake, and resume working side by side with a man I'm living with. Did I get that right?"

"Well…yeah. It'll be great, Brent. You'll see. We can have great parties at the lake house. Just last weekend, Ev and I hosted—"

"No. I don't want to hear about your parties, Kenn. I told you before, I'm through with that life. I want to settle down. Have a home. Maybe kids one day." He rubbed a hand over his face and tried to find words beneath this new heartbreak. "I wanted that with you."

"Wanted. Past tense."

Brent gave him credit for picking up on the important part of what he'd said. "Yes. Past tense."

"You've met someone? Already?" His voice rose to a high pitch. "What. The. Fuck? You've been there, what, six, eight weeks?"

Four. But who was counting? "And you're fucking Everett."

"Yeah, but I've known Ev for, like, forever."

And it felt as if he'd known Rick forever. "I've got to go. I have a client waiting." Brent swallowed hard then pushed the painful words past his lips. "Don't call me again, Kenn." He forced himself to carefully replace the handset in the cradle, when he wanted to slam it down hard enough to break it in half.

Rocking back in his chair, he scrubbed both palms over his face and blew out a heavy breath. Kenn had ruined any chance he had to return to Houston and resume any part of his old life. And he'd blown, pardon the pun, any chance of being happy in Willowbrook. *Fuck!*

Jean's voice came over the intercom. "Mr. Whitehall, the Wilsons are here to see you."

Standing, he smoothed his jacket and straightened his glasses as he mentally went over what he knew about this next appointment. A family trust, if he recalled correctly. The couple had recently inherited some property and wanted to preserve it for their kids. He greeted the couple and, once they were all seated, pulled out a note pad and focused on helping someone else instead of obsessing about the shambles he'd made of his personal life.

The afternoon went by in a flash as he consulted with clients, one after the other. When Jean appeared in his door late in the day, he sighed with relief at her words. "Well, that was the last one. Unless you need something else, I'm going to head home now. I need some time to decompress before Jake's party." He'd forgotten all about it. "So? Do you need anything?"

"Nah. I'm good." He waved her off.

She pushed away from the doorframe where she'd been leaning. "Okeydokey, then. I'll see you there?"

Hell, no. He caught the words before they formed then forced a smile to his lips. "Sure." Any other answer would require an explanation, and he didn't want to get into his personal life with his secretary. It would be easier to make an excuse for not attending after the fact.

"I'm out of here." She wiggled her fingers at him. "Tootles."

As soon as Jean turned her key in the lock on the front door, he tossed his glasses across his desk and let his body go limp in the chair. What a fucking day. It was over, finally. He'd go home, heat some leftovers for dinner, and take a long soak in the tub. With a little luck, he'd be fast asleep before Rick got home from the party. Tomorrow, he'd get up and out of the house before his landlord. The plan would buy him another twenty-four hours before he had to face Rick.

His phone vibrated in his pocket as he wearily dropped into his car. Stifling a groan, he pushed the Accept Call button as he fired the powerful engine to life. "Sis. What's up?"

"I'm sorry, Brent."

He loved his youngest sister, he really did, but Meg had a flare for the dramatic. He rolled his eyes and cranked the heater up to full blast. "What do you have to be sorry for?" A long silence from the other end put him on alert. He straightened his spine. "Megan Renee. You better tell me right now or I'll—"

"Don't you dare tell Mom about my trip to New Orleans. I swear, Brent, I'll kill you if you do."

His sister had trusted him with her shocking secret, and, as her lawyer, he couldn't legally disclose anything she'd told him, but he wasn't going to remind her of that—not when she was withholding something from him. "Spill, Megs."

She sighed loud enough he took the phone from his ear and switched to speaker mode. "Okay. Okay. But promise me you won't be mad at me."

"I'm not promising anything, egg head." He hoped using the nickname he'd given her when he was eleven and her eight would loosen her tongue.

"Jerk."

"Butt fungus."

Another long silence. He could picture her biting her lower lip, her brows knit as she worked up the courage to admit to whatever she'd done. As a child, she'd gotten into more trouble than anyone he knew, and it hadn't stopped once she reached adulthood. Trouble seemed to find her the way tornadoes found trailer parks. Often with similar results. "I called to warn you."

"Of?" He drew out the single syllable.

"I think Kenn is coming to see you."

He closed his eyes, remembering the call from his former lover earlier. "Why would you think that?"

"Because he called me and asked for your address."

"You told him?" He hated how his voice rose there at the end, but he couldn't help it.

"Well, you didn't tell me it was a secret, and he told me how much he missed you. Said he'd made a mistake."

Shit. "What time did this conversation happen?"

"This morning. I tried to call you when I thought you'd be a lunch, but it went straight to voicemail."

"I was with a client," he lied.

"I'm sorry, Brent. I should have asked you before giving out your private information. But it was Kenn. Besides, he knew the name of the hotel you'd been staying in. Even had the room number right. I figured if you'd told him that, then you wouldn't mind him knowing where you were now."

It was sound logic, if he'd told Kenn those details, but he hadn't. *I should have stayed in bed this morning.* "No worries, egg head. I'm not mad at you." Another lie but a little one. He was peeved, and that was at least one step below full-out mad.

A glance up told him the defroster had cleared the windshield. "I gotta go, sis. My boss is having a party tonight." He wasn't going, but she didn't need to know that.

"You're sure you aren't mad at me?"

"Positive." He put the car in gear and checked the rearview mirror. "Now, I really need to go."

"Go," she said, sounding less stressed and more like the bubbly person she was. "Have fun tonight."

The line went dead. He backed out of his parking space and turned the car toward his temporary home. He made a mental note to ask Jean tomorrow if she'd had any luck finding him a new place.

It took longer to warm up the car than to make the drive to Rick's house. As he neared the perfect little cottage, he noted a familiar silhouette sitting on the top step of the porch. Rick's beat-up old truck was gone, giving him a measure of relief, so he pulled into the driveway and got out. Approaching the front door, keys in hand in case his landlord had locked the door for a change, he stopped when his visitor stood.

He let his chin drop to his chest. *Fuck, how is this my life?*

"Brent?"

Clutching the keys in his fist until the sharp edges cut into his skin, he lifted his gaze to the man who had cut his heart out and stomped on it for good measure. He wore his usual work clothes, jeans aged to perfection and a long-sleeved T-shirt beneath a butter-soft leather bomber-style jacket. Years of familiarity allowed him to see the fatigue in his eyes and in the lines of his face. "Kenn. What are you doing here?" *How the hell did he get here so soon? Hadn't he been in Houston when we talked a few hours ago?* "How did you get here?"

"I needed to see you." He couldn't say the same, so he didn't. "You look good. Small-town life agrees with you."

That was bullshit if he'd ever heard it. *I look like hell, and Willowbrook is killing me.* He'd caught a glimpse of himself in the rearview mirror. His eyes were red. His hair in disarray from running his fingers through it. He needed a shave and a frown had carved deep brackets around his mouth and between his brows. Choosing to ignore the absurd comment, he stalked past his unwanted guest and tried the doorknob. When it turned easily, he silently cursed Rick Ingram for being such a trusting bastard.

Willowbrook might be relatively crime-free, but you never knew when some asshole from out of town would drop by. Lucky for him, it never would have occurred to this particular asshole to check the door. Where he came from, no one left their doors unlocked.

Standing in the open portal, he half turned to the man standing behind him. "I've got some place to be, and I'm running late." More lies, but he needed Kenn to leave sooner rather than later.

"That's okay. We can talk while you get ready."

Motherfucker. The man couldn't take a hint. Resigned to letting him have his say, he huffed out a breath then invited the man in.

"Shut the door behind you," he said, shedding his overcoat as he stomped down the hall to his room. He tossed the coat on the bed then toed off his dress shoes while he shrugged his suit coat off.

"Nice room." Sarcasm dripped from Kenn's words.

"It's a place to sleep until my new apartment is finished."

"I thought you wanted a house. One like this one." He listed all the things Brent had said he wanted in his new home. Rick's house checked off every box.

Lord, save me. "I do, but there aren't any available at the moment, so I'm renting a room from my boss's brother."

Kenn's posture in the doorway grew rigid. "He's the guy your sleeping with?"

"That's none of your business."

"Are you sure, Brent?"

No matter how bad things seemed at this moment, he hadn't changed his mind about leaving the big city for a small town. It sucked that he hadn't found a house of his own, but he would. Eventually. After what happened that morning, Rick would probably work night and day to get the apartment done and Brent out of his house.

He fixed his gaze on his guest. "I'm sure. I asked you to come with me, to make a life with me, and you declined. I might not be settled yet, but I'm happy here. I like my job. I like this town. It's a community, something a big city can never be."

Kenn's shoulders slumped, and he dropped his gaze to the floor. He was no longer trying to hide his exhaustion. "I came to say I'm sorry, Brent. I made a mistake letting you go. I thought you'd find this place boring and come back in a few weeks, but I got tired of waiting, so I tried to push you."

"That's what all that shit was about, Everett?" He pulled a flannel shirt from the closet, and a pair of jeans from a drawer.

"That was bullshit. I haven't been with anyone since you left. I thought I could make you jealous, but then you said you'd moved on, and…shit…I knew I'd fucked up, big-time."

"So, you aren't sleeping with my former coworker, and you aren't interested in a threesome with him?"

His gaze shot up to Brent's. "No." Hands he'd had tucked in his pockets rose to a defensive position. "I swear. I said that shit to get a reaction out of you."

Brent dropped his trousers, pulled his jeans on then switched his dress shirt and tie for the more casual shirt he'd laid out. It was time to put an end to the conversation. "I'm not going back to Houston, or to you, Kenn."

"I know that now. That's why I'm here. Show me this town you like so much. I'm miserable without you, baby. I think I could be happy anywhere you are."

He tucked his shirt in then bent to find a pair of casual loafers he'd stuffed under the bed for lack of another place to put them. "You aren't listening," he said, leveraging to his feet. "You and I are finished."

"I heard you. Loud and clear, but you aren't hearing me. Houston isn't the same without you. The parties aren't as much fun, and it turns out, most of *our* friends were *your* friends."

Shit. I shouldn't feel sorry for him, but I do. As a military brat, he'd moved around a lot and had learned, out of necessity, to make friends. Kenn was an only child and had never lived anywhere but Houston where his parents were both professors at a prestigious private college. To say his social skills were stunted was an understatement.

"Where you going? Are you meeting your new lover there?"

There is no new lover. Not after what happened this morning. But Kenn didn't need to know the details of his sordid sex life. However, what would it hurt to rub Rick's nose in the shitshow he'd created by staying in the closet until the door hinges were almost too rusty to open? The least the man could have done was call him and let him know how it went with his brother, or brothers, as the case might be. He got the sense the brothers grim were a tight bunch, despite the secret the youngest had been keeping most of his life. He hoped they'd accepted the news with open minds, but he wouldn't know unless he walked into the lion's den on his own since Rick apparently wasn't going to talk about it. Decision made, he slipped a worn leather belt through the loops on his pants. "My boss and his wife are having a gender reveal party tonight. Wanna go?"

Kenn straightened his shoulders. "You want me to go with you?"

Not really, but, "Yeah. Might as well. Knowing Jake, nearly everyone in town will be there."

CHAPTER NINETEEN

Hoping to avoid Brent, Rick knocked off work early, went home, showered, and changed then lit out for Jake's house. His brother, still in jeans and barefoot, met him at the door.

"You're early."

He shrugged and stepped past him into the foyer. "Found a good place to stop, so I thought I'd come see if I could help out, but from the trucks in the driveway, you've got it handled."

"Yeah." Jake glanced at the empty porch before shutting the door. "I didn't want Sunny to overdo, so I had the entire thing catered."

Rick nodded. "I'll be the official taste-tester, then. Wouldn't want to serve something sub-standard to your guests."

"Speaking of guests, where's Brent?"

He didn't want to admit he didn't ask his tenant/lover to come with him, so he lied through his teeth. "Said he had something else tonight."

Jake strode past him, and Rick followed. "What the hell could he have to do in Willowbrook on a weeknight?"

"Work, maybe? You're his boss. You know him better than I do." Jake stopped so fast, Rick almost plowed into him. The look he shot over his shoulder reminded Rick of their father when he had a burr up his butt about something. "Don't fucking look at me that way." He lowered his voice. "We had sex, Jake. Just sex. We don't share our plans with each other." That much was true.

His older brother shook his head then strode off. Rick let out a relieved breath then took off after him. He caught up with him in the kitchen. Jake's wife, Sunny, rose from her spot at the island to give Rick a hug.

"I'm so glad you're here." She smiled up at him. "I know you're busier than a one-armed bartender on ten-cent beer night, but Jake needs help with the nursery. Can you take a look?"

"I've got it," Jake protested.

"No. You don't." Ignoring her husband, she grabbed Rick's wrist and tugged him down the hallway leading to the bedrooms. Jake trailed behind them, grumbling about being underappreciated. Rick smiled to himself knowing his brother's complaints were all for show. The man didn't have a handyman bone in his body. "It doesn't need much. Just some paint and a closet organizer, I think." She dragged him into the bedroom across the hall from the master suite. "What do you think?"

Rick took in the little-used room with its dull beige paint, standard small closet, and unimaginative lighting. "You keeping the carpet?"

Sunny bit her bottom lip and shrugged. "I don't know. Am I?"

Rick laughed. "No. I can match the hardwood in the rest of the house, if you want."

"I want," she replied, a giant smile on her face. "And could we change the overhead light? I saw this really nice chandelier the other day…"

"Honey," Jake interrupted. "Rick has a lot on his plate."

"It's a small room," he countered. Even if he had to do the work after hours, he couldn't disappoint his sister-in-law, not when she gave him that lost puppy dog look. "It won't take long. Why don't you show me the light you want, and I bet you have a closet organizer picked out, too."

"How did you know?"

He shrugged, suppressing the laughter bubbling inside him. "Just a hunch." Jake had stopped by several times in the last few weeks ostensibly to talk about the upcoming apartment renovation when Rick suspected he'd wanted an excuse to get out of working on the nursery. As they filed out of the room, he clapped his brother on the back. "Don't worry. I've got this. It's going to cost you, big-time, but I've got it."

The elbow he received to the ribs was as good a thank you as he was going to get from his big brother. It would do. Guests began arriving shortly after their nursery consultation. The expectant couple had invited a houseful, and Rick found himself relaxing, enjoying catching up with old friends. He was part of a group listening to Hank Travis tell a story from BlackWing's latest European tour when Will pulled him aside. "Where's your boy toy? Kenzie wants to meet him."

Rick's gaze slid from his brother to the woman standing beside him. Will's girlfriend smiled up at him. "I hope you don't mind. Will told me what happened."

He did mind which was the point of keeping his secret in the first place, but his impulsiveness had created a gap in the careful seal he'd placed around his privacy. It was his lousy luck his brother had stumbled his way in. Now, every goddamn person on the planet was going to know his most private business. Still, it wasn't Kenzie's fault, so he reached deep for the patience he'd honed on countless missions overseas and lied through his teeth. "No, I don't mind, but I'd appreciate it if you both"—he shot Will a pointed look—"kept it to yourself."

"Of course we will," Kenzie promised. "It's really none of our business, but we both wanted you to know it makes no difference to us. You're Will's brother. Full stop. But…" She stretched the word out. "I missed meeting him at Jake's wedding. Did he come with you?"

"No. I'm not sure where he is." Truth without admitting anything. He'd learned a few things from his lawyer brother.

Someone touched his elbow. He glanced over his shoulder to see Jake's legal secretary and a familiar older man standing there. *Shit.* "Jean," he greeted her with a hug. He'd known her most of his life. She'd worked for his asshole dad before his death and had always been good to him and his brothers. She baked a mean Snickerdoodle, too. He shook hands with her husband, a retired Air Force pilot who operated the small, local airstrip outside of town. "Lowell. Nice to see you again. It's been a while. You remember my brother, Will?" He brought his middle brother into the conversation then introduced Will's fiancée. Will and Lowell struck up a conversation regarding the airstrip he managed and something about the Yankee billionaire who had purchased it a couple of years ago and put it back on the map. Rick was thanking his lucky stars for the change of topic when Jean drew him aside.

"Where's Brent?"

Why did everyone here expect Brent to be glued to his side? He shot a glare at his chatty middle brother whose disrespect of personal boundaries had started this whole mess then glanced around the room as if looking for the man in question. "Don't know. Did you look outside?"

Jake had heaters set up on the patio for those who wanted to catch some fresh air. The underwater lights and steam rising from the heated pool created a mystical atmosphere that had drawn some of the guests outside.

"No. I thought he'd be with you."

"Why would he be with me?"

"Jake told me he was coming with you, and when I spoke with Brent about the party, he said he'd be here."

Shit. Shit. Shit. He'd known better than to hope Jake hadn't invited his new employee. From the looks of the crowded room, he'd invited everyone in town. Or not. Most folks in Willowbrook didn't think they needed an invitation. If there was a party going on, they considered themselves invited. The only time he could recall security being tight for an event was Jake's wedding, and even then, his brother had provided an extensive list of party crashers who were allowed in without showing an invitation. Almost everyone on the list had attended.

Avoiding eye contact with Jean, he went with a version of the truth. "He didn't come with me." It came out sharper than he intended causing the older woman to take a step back.

"Okay. Sorry I asked." She steered her husband away.

He owed her an apology, but it could wait. Jake and Sunny sidled up next to him. "What did you do to her?"

"Nothing. She was being nosy."

"So you rubbed her nose in it?"

"Something like that." Giving most of the room his back, he addressed his sister-in-law. "Nice party."

Her smile lit their corner of the room, and he didn't miss the way the hand that wasn't clinging to his brother cradled her ever-growing baby bump. "Thanks. Have you had something to eat? The barbequed brisket is to die for."

He returned her smile. Jake was a lucky man. His wife was beyond beautiful, and her name fit her personality to a T. "Is there any left? I've been trying to get to the buffet for a while now and keep getting waylaid."

"There's plenty. Jake ordered enough to feed an army." She uncoupled from her husband and took Rick's arm instead. "Come on. Everyone knows not to get in between a pregnant woman and a buffet table."

As she led him off, the crowd parting like the Red Sea, he glanced over his shoulder at his brother. Jake saluted him with the beer he'd held in his free hand then ambled off to speak with another guest.

"This is my second pass," Sunny confided as they loaded up their plates with brisket, baked beans, potato salad, and cornbread. "But don't tell anybody, okay?"

"Your secret is safe with me."

"I'm sure it is," she deadpanned. "You're like a vault."

He followed her through the kitchen to the laundry/mudroom. "Shut the door, please?"

Rick shut the door, sealing them away from the noise and crowds. "You okay?" She sat on the bench near the door leading to the garage and dug into her food.

"I'm fine. Just wanted a chance to eat before my food gets cold." She practically inhaled half of her slice of cornbread. "This is amazing, don't you think?"

"It sure is," he replied, not bothering to taste it himself. The catering was from a local barbeque place he'd eaten at dozens of times. People came from all around to sample their barbeque.

"I'll give you one thing about Texas. The cuisine here is stupendous. I've gained more weight than I should have, but everything here is so good." The transplant from New York shoveled in a bite of potato salad, humming her enthusiastic approval of the side dish. "So, want to tell me what's going on between you and Brent?"

Her abrupt change of subject caused him to swallow wrong. After nearly coughing up a lung, he washed everything down with a giant gulp of the sweet tea he'd snagged on the way to their hideout. "What?" he croaked.

"Don't pretend ignorance. Jake told me everything."

God, save me from busybodies. "There's nothing going on. It was sex between consenting adults."

She forked up a slice of brisket but didn't immediately eat it. She shook her head. "I don't believe you. You've gone to a lot of trouble to keep your sexuality private. To be caught the way you were…it doesn't make sense."

He'd placed his plate on top of the washing machine. Appetite lost, he shoved it away. "It's not like I was blowing him on the sidewalk. We were in *my* kitchen. In *my* house, where I have every right to expect privacy."

Chewing, Sunny nodded. After taking a sip from the water bottle she'd brought with her, she sliced off another bite of the barbequed meat. "You're absolutely right about the expectation of privacy, but still—you're a Marine. You didn't survive multiple deployments by not being aware of your surroundings and potential threats."

"Your point?"

"You were distracted. I'm thinking the distraction had to be more than sex. You're a grown man, presumably capable of curbing your appetites unless…you couldn't help yourself."

Bracing his hips against the washer, he crossed his arms over his chest and studied the herringbone tile pattern on the floor. "I don't know what you want me to say, Sunny. I wanted to suck his dick, so I did. If Will had respected my privacy, no one but Brent and me would know. I wanted to keep it that way."

"Well, that ship has sailed." She stuffed her face with potato salad, chewed, and swallowed. "I really didn't drag you in here to pry into your private life. What I wanted to say is, we all love you, and if Brent makes you happy, that's great. If not, then that's okay, too. Jake said he'd fire him if he hurt you, but since you're adamant it's only sex, then there isn't much chance of him breaking your heart. Not that Jake would actually fire him. He's too good at his job." Polishing off the last bite on her plate, she stood. As she passed by him, she patted him on the shoulder. "Glad we had this little chat. We'll be cutting the cake soon, so finish up and get out there."

The door shut behind her, leaving Rick alone with his turbulent thoughts. He'd once thought being out of the closet would be so much easier. No more secrets. Nothing to hide. Piece of rainbow-tinted cake. Except it wasn't easier. Now that his siblings and their women knew he *had* a sex life, they felt entitled to the details. Well, fuck them. Maybe it had been the isolation this past weekend, or the loneliness he'd experienced since Dave's defection that had made him think he could have a relationship with Brent. Whatever the cause of his stupid thoughts along those lines, reality set in the second his brother caught him with Brent's dick down his throat. He'd come to his senses. His brothers still loved him, as he knew they would.

It was the rest of the world he wasn't ready to face. Brent made no effort to hide his sexual orientation. If he was seen around town with the openly gay man, the news would travel so fast, it would set the grapevine on fire. Everyone would know his private business. He'd be labeled *different*. Some wouldn't care. Others would care too much. He and his brothers had been the source of enough gossip growing up. Giving them more fuel as an adult made him want to vomit.

"It's fucking none of their business," he exclaimed to the ceiling.

A knock sounded on the door a split second before the handle turned and Will peeked inside. "Sunny said for you to get your ass out here so they can cut this fucking cake. Her words, not mine."

He couldn't keep Jake's wife waiting. No telling what she'd do if he didn't join the other guests in time to see if they were having a boy or a girl. He gathered his plate and drink. "I'm coming."

"That's what *he* said." Will winked at him, adding the *cha-ching* to his lame joke.

When Will turned his back, Rick allowed himself a smile. "You're just jealous because *she* never says it."

The guests had gathered in a loose circle around a giant sheet cake that had been set up on a table in the living room. The brothers took up a spot on the outer ring where they could see the happy couple.

Will smirked. "*She* says it *multiple* times every day."

He nudged Will in the ribs. "TMI, brother."

Though his food had grown cold, Rick quickly cleaned his plate anyway then stepped away to toss the soiled paper plate into one of the large trash cans set up in the kitchen for the occasion. He was returning to his spot next to Will when a shiver of awareness caused him to scan the crowd. Like Sunny had said, he hadn't stayed alive by sticking his head in the sand, and he never ignored his gut when it told him something was wrong. He just wished his gut had spoken up this morning. Damned unreliable alarm system. Still, he hung back, his gaze quickly assessing the gathering for whatever had made his hackles rise.

It didn't take him long to spy Brent among the guests. His breath caught in his lungs, and his dick twitched to life. The last time he'd seen him he'd been tucking his dick back in his pants as he practically ran out of the room, leaving Rick to deal with Will. It was a chickenshit thing to do, but Rick hadn't exactly asked him to stay, either.

His tenant had swapped out his fancy suit for jeans, and the collar of a plaid shirt peeked from the neck of a heavy, cream-colored sweater. There wasn't anything special about the outfit, but Brent wore it like a fashion model. Rick's fingers itched to toss the bulky clothes off to get to the ripped body beneath. To wrap his lips around his cock and finish what he'd started earlier. To hear his name grunted out as the man dropped his civilized veneer and came.

Jean approached Brent, her husband in tow, blocking his sightline and ripping him out of his inappropriate musings. She made the introductions then Brent half turned and, with the familiarity of a longtime friend, took the hand of the dark-haired man on his other side and pulled him front and center.

Rick's feet grew heavy, like he'd stepped in quick-drying cement, and his heart lodged in his throat, blocking his airway. *What. The. Fuck?* He'd brought a date? *What. The.* Ever-loving. *Fuck?*

The sound of silver tapping crystal drew his attention away from Brent and his date to Sunny and Jake who'd gravitated to the center of the circle. Jake cleared his throat. "We'd like to thank you all for coming out tonight on such short notice. After the record snowfall over the weekend, we thought you could all use a night out, so we threw this together on the fly," he said. Sunny elbowed him in the ribs. Jake grunted, a smile coming over his face. "That's a lie. We were going to do this next week, but my lovely wife couldn't wait any longer to find out if she's carrying our son or our daughter. Some nonsense about what color to paint the nursery."

The comment earned him another elbow to the ribs. Sunny gave him a long-suffering look then addressed the gathering. "Don't believe a word out of his mouth. He's the one who can't stand not knowing. He's the one to blame for dragging you out for barbeque and cake on a cold Monday night."

Several comments rose from the crowd. "Anytime."

"Not a problem."

"Cake? Did someone say cake?" Laughter rose from the guests.

Jake raised his hand. "So, without further ado..."

They joined hands like they'd done a few months ago at their wedding and sliced into the cake. Sunny let out a gasp, tears instantly brightening her eyes. Beaming, she turned her face up to Jake's. His brother's smile was as big as Texas as he bent to place a kiss on his wife's lips.

"Well?" some jackass yelled.

"Should we tell them?" Jake asked Sunny.

His sister-in-law nodded. "Yeah, we should."

Together, they grasped the knife, carved out the corner piece, and slid it around, revealing the bright-pink center. "It's a girl!" they said in unison.

Kenzie, Will's fiancée rushed in to slice the cake into serving pieces while Jake and Sunny accepted congratulations and kept the cake line moving.

CHAPTER TWENTY

He sensed Rick's gaze on him but refused to hunt for him in the crowd. As he smiled and introduced Kenn to the few people he knew, he mentally told his landlord to go fuck himself. It was one thing to be caught with his dick down someone's throat before breakfast. It was another to have the owner of said throat project his shame on him. They hadn't been doing anything wrong, and they'd been in their own kitchen, for crying out loud.

He got it. He really did. Rick had been in the closet for a long time, and he'd gone to great lengths to keep the metaphorical door locked tight. It wasn't Brent's fault the ass hadn't laid down the law with his family—or at the very least, changed the locks on his physical doors. That shit landed square on Rick's shoulders.

Was he sorry Rick's brothers had found out the way they had? Yes. But he wasn't sorry Rick's secret was out. He was a grown-ass man. It was about time he owned his sexuality, though, a part of him wished he'd had the chance to tell his family in his own way. Seeing his presumably hetero brother sucking dick had to have been a shock for Will. Which was why he tensed as the other man approached.

"Brent." Will Ingram held out his hand. "Glad you could make it. I know Jake will be happy to see you."

He took the middle Ingram brother's hand in his and shook it. "I wouldn't have missed it for the world. I thought Jake was happy on his wedding day, but the day he told me about the baby, his feet barely touched the ground."

"I know." Will smiled. "The fucker is crazy happy."

The sound of a throat being cleared drew his attention to the man standing beside him. "Will Ingram, this is an old friend of mine, Kenneth Westinghouse. I hope Jake doesn't mind an extra guest. Kenn stopped by for a visit, and I didn't want to disappoint my boss, so I brought him along."

Will's smile froze as he sized Kenn up then, he gave a slight nod and held his hand out in a friendly gesture. The two men shook hands. "Welcome, Kenn. You haven't met my older brother yet, but I can assure you, Jake won't mind another party crasher. Hell, half the people here weren't invited. It's the way things are in Willowbrook. We're all one big, happy family."

"Speaking of Jake," Brent said, "I need to go razz him about having a daughter."

Will pointed over his shoulder. "He and Sunny are still holding court by the cake. Better hurry if you want a piece."

Once they were out of earshot, Kenn grabbed his sleeve and pulled him to a stop. "Was that W.H. Ingram? The artist?" he asked in a near whisper.

"Yeah. I think he signs his latest work as William H. Ingram though. Don't ask me why. Jake handles all his legal affairs. Why?"

"Is he the one you're fucking?"

"What? No. He's engaged. His fiancée is around here somewhere."

"Honest? I wouldn't be all that upset if you were fucking him. That's W.H. Ingram! I'd fuck him in a heartbeat. Lord, that man is sexy. And talented. He's your boss's brother?"

"Middle brother. There's another Ingram. Jake's the oldest of the three."

"Let me guess." His gaze raked the crowd that had dispersed some to enjoy their pink cake. "It's the sexy-as-hell guy over there giving us both the stink-eye, right? He looks like a bigger, badder version of William. Tell me he's gay. Please."

He didn't need to look to know exactly who Kenn referred to. There was only one sexy male in the room who would be giving them the stink-eye. It was petty of him, but a thrill shot through him at the thought of having rattled Rick's cage enough to get a public reaction out of him. Maybe bringing his former lover along hadn't been such a bad idea after all. "Fuck, Kenn. What's the matter with you? The Ingram brothers are off-limits. All of them."

"Then I nailed it. He's the other brother. What's his name? I'd ride that all day long and twice on Sunday."

Kenn's crude remark made Brent think about the various ways Rick had fucked him over the weekend and how twice hadn't been anywhere near the count on Sunday. The memories brought a wave of heat to his cheeks and made his dick throb for a repeat. Or at least a conclusion to what they'd started that morning. "Cut it out, Kenn."

At Brent's sharp reprimand, the cartoonist cut him a glance. "Oh. My. God. It's him, isn't it? He's the one your fucking?" He cocked his head toward the man he'd been ogling. "He's the reason you won't move back to Houston? The reason you won't be with me?"

"No," he lied.

"Then why is he looking at me like he wants to kill me?"

He didn't dare glance Rick's way. And even though he'd brought Kenn to the party as a fuck-you to Rick, he couldn't bear to see the lips that had been wrapped around his cock less than twelve hours ago turned down in disapproval. "It's your imagination. Come on. Let's say hi to Jake and his wife and get the fuck out of here."

~ ~ ~

"That was awkward."

"Do me a favor, Kenn, and shut the fuck up." Brent white-knuckled the Corvette steering wheel. The car seemed to know its way to Dallas without any input from him. A good thing since he was too busy cursing himself, the man in the passenger seat, and Rick Fucking Ingram to pay attention to the road.

"I will if you tell me where we're going."

"Airport."

"My return ticket isn't good until day after tomorrow. Why don't we go back to your place?"

He ground his teeth in an effort to keep from saying something he'd regret later on. Once he gained control of his words, he carefully enunciated his thoughts. "We aren't going back to my place because I don't want you there. There aren't any spare beds and you aren't sleeping with me."

"I could sleep with your roomie."

His molars were going to be dust soon. They were miles from their destination, but he started paying attention to the billboards, looking for the first motel, hotel, or hovel where he could dump his passenger. "Don't even think it," he ground out.

"I knew it."

Kenn's words lacked the teasing tone he'd adopted earlier, causing Brent to glance at him. The light over an exit ramp briefly illuminated the man's features. Where he'd been a bright balloon, trying to tease a positive response out of Brent, he looked spent. Dejected. *Welcome to the crowd.* "Knew what?"

"You're hung up on Rick Ingram. Your landlord." In his periphery, he saw the man shake his head. "How cliché can you get, Brent?"

"Don't say another fucking word or I'll pull over and leave your ass on the side of the road."

"He's a Neanderthal for Christ's sake, Brent! You don't belong with someone like him. Does he even know how to read?"

Before he was through spewing crap from his mouth, Brent pulled the car to a stop on the shoulder of the road. "Out. Get. The. Fuck. *Out!*"

"No. Not until you listen to me."

Short of physically hauling his ass out, there wasn't much he could do but let him have his say. He shoved the transmission into Park and turned on his flashers. "Say what you want to say, Kenn, then I don't want to hear another word out of you. Okay?"

"Okay." His former lover tugged at his jacket, settling into his seat. "I don't know what's going on with you, Brent. We had something good in Houston. We were happy. At least I was, and I thought you were, too. Then this offer came up in Willowbrook and everything changed. You changed. I get it. I do. I've dated military brats before. They either can't settle down or it's all they think about. I thought you were settled.

You had a great job and a kick-ass apartment. You had friends. You had me." He sighed.

Brent remained quiet, his gaze focused on a reflective mile marker post in the distance, waiting for his passenger to get everything he wanted to say off his chest.

Kenn shifted in his seat, and Brent could feel the man's gaze on him. "You have nothing in common with him. Can't you see that? I heard someone at the party talking about how he renovated her kitchen. For Christ's sake, Brent, he's a construction worker!"

That was it. Maybe Rick didn't want him enough to be seen with him in public, but he wasn't going to let anyone talk smack about him. "Shut. The. Fuck. Up." He forced his gaze on the man he'd once thought he'd spend the rest of his life with. Light from the dashboard instruments touched on his soft facial features—such a contrast from the way moonlight off the snow had softened Rick's sharp edges. How had he ever thought Kenn was the one for him? "You don't know anything about him. He's a former Marine who survived multiple deployments to war zones and came home to build his own renovation business from scratch. He might not have an Ivy League education, but he's not stupid. And I'd trust him with my life." Unlike you, went unsaid.

They'd been mugged once on vacation in New Orleans, and Brent had done more to fight back than Kenn, who'd cowered on the sidewalk and pissed his pants. Rick Ingram might not want anything to do with him, but he knew down to the marrow of his bones the man would put his own life on the line to protect him.

"He makes me feel safe." He wasn't sure where the thought had come from, but he knew it to be true.

He put the car in Drive and took his foot off the brake. "There's a chain motel at the next exit. We aren't far from the airport. I'm sure they have a shuttle, or you can call a car service to get you there."

To Kenn's credit, he didn't say another word until they pulled up beneath the motel's portico and he'd retrieved his backpack, the only luggage he'd brought with him, from the backseat. "I'm sorry, Brent. I shouldn't have come, but I had to see you…give it one more try."

"I get it, but I hope you understand now. I'm not going back to Houston. Even if things don't work out with Rick, I'm going to stay in Willowbrook. It feels like home." He'd never thought those words about any place he'd ever lived, much less said them aloud. The truth of them warmed a cold place in his heart. It was a night for truths, he supposed.

Kenn nodded then, without a second look, exited the car. The glass doors parted automatically at his approach. Brent waited until he'd checked in and walked toward the elevators before he drove across the street to a similar hotel and booked himself a room for the night.

CHAPTER TWENTY-ONE

Rick's truck was gone when Brent pulled up in front of the house the following morning. He mentally congratulated himself on his timing. He still wasn't ready to face his landlord, and after parading his "date" around at Jake's party, he was sure Rick had plenty to say to him. None of which could be good. He'd be lucky if he still had a place to live this time tomorrow. No, his best plan of action was to avoid Rick Ingram at all costs, for as long as possible. Give him time to cool down. Time to process what it meant to be out of the closet, even if it was only to family members.

He parked in the driveway and cut through the backyard to the kitchen door. He'd skipped the free breakfast at the hotel in favor of getting out of there before Kenn got out of bed. Since his former lover rarely got out of bed before noon, there was little chance of him seeing Brent's car in the lot across the street, but it was a chance he hadn't been willing to take. Better to head home—yeah, Willowbrook was home—as early as possible.

First things first. He popped a pod into the coffee maker, pulled a container of cream from the refrigerator while his first cup brewed. He normally didn't drink more than one cup in the morning, but today was definitely a two-cup day. He was in the process of removing a slice of bread from the wrapper when the back door opened. Certain Rick had returned for some reason, he didn't bother to look up. Even when the door slammed shut, rattling the windows and jump-starting his heart, he refused to look up. If the man wanted to talk, he could talk. Brent was a good listener, had to be in his job. Clients often didn't know how to verbalize what they wanted, so a good lawyer had to listen close and cull out the important parts of what they were saying. He'd let him have his say then he had a few things he wanted to get off his mind.

The fact that Rick hadn't spoken barely registered until he turned to put his bread slices into the toaster. Movement near the door drew his gaze. He gasped. The bread slid from his fingers that had gone numb at the sight of a woman standing there with a wide grin on her face.

"You really should lock your doors." As she spoke, she raised her hand above the level of the counter. A gun. Brent stumbled back.

"Whoa. Whoa. You can have anything you want." He held both hands up, palms out in an effort to placate the intruder. "I've got a little cash in my wallet. You can have it. I'll give you the pin for my debit card. Anything you want. There's stuff here you can pawn." She had to be a drug addict in need of money. Right? What else could this be about? Hell, he'd help her load up her car with shit if she'd just leave him alone.

She took another step into the kitchen, brandishing the weapon in his direction. "I want your worthless brother," she said. "He owes me."

Brother? "Wha-what? Wh-who?"

"William. Your brother. Where is he?"

God, he wished she'd quit waving that thing around. Between the gun and the fact he hadn't had any caffeine yet, he was having a hard time deciphering her words. "He's…not here."

"I heard he was living here."

"Uh. Not anymore?"

"He talked about this shit town all the time. I'd bet he didn't go far. Call him. Get him over here."

"Ca-call him?" If he got out of this alive, he was going to carve Rick Ingram a new asshole for never locking his doors.

"Call him. You've got a phone, don't you?"

He nodded. *I've got a phone. Where is it?* He patted all his pockets and came up empty. Oh, right. The jacket he'd shrugged off as soon as he'd walked in the door. "It's in my coat." He gestured toward the article of clothing draped over the back of a nearby chair.

The woman used her gun hand to wave him toward the garment. "Get it, but if you try anything funny, I'll shoot you and call him myself."

"Okay. No funny stuff." There was nothing funny about this shit.

He hated the way his hands shook as he searched his coat pockets for the slender device. There were any number of things in the kitchen he could use as a weapon. If he could get to his coffee, he could throw that in her face, but she'd stepped between him and the coffee maker. He could toss his coat at her and run, but that would only be a moment's distraction, and she might decide to shoot first and untangle herself second.

As his hand closed around the plastic case, he considered throwing the phone at her. Only he'd never been any good at throwing. He'd been decent with a baseball bat, but he'd been so lousy at throwing, he'd given up on playing the game. Again, if he managed to hit her, it wouldn't buy him enough time to get to the front door, much less out of the house before she shot his ass. Better to play along until help arrived.

"Got it." He held his cell phone up for her to see.

"Call him. Now."

"Okay. Okay." He didn't have William's number, but she didn't need to know that. *She thinks I'm Rick.*

He brought up his contact list. It took two tries to key in Rick's name. When the number came up, he pressed the Call button and hoped to hell his landlord was over being mad at him enough to take the call. If he wasn't, maybe he could hit her over the head with the cast-iron skillet he'd left out on the stove. If he could reach it before she shot him.

"It's ringing." He glanced up at his captor and mentally tabulated a list of all the crimes she was guilty of so far. Trespassing. Kidnapping. He hoped to hell murder didn't get added to the list.

~ ~ ~

Rick slipped his phone from his pocket and sighed. He wasn't in the mood to talk to his tenant. The fucker. Who did he think he was, bringing a date to Jake's party not even twelve hours after Rick had sucked his dick? He hadn't come home last night, and knowing he'd spent the night with another man chapped Rick's butt. If he was calling to apologize, he could save his breath. He didn't want to hear it.

He stuck the phone in his pocket and measured the front window, noting the measurement on his old-fashioned notepad. When his phone vibrated, indicating a message had been left, he let loose a string of profanity harsh enough to peel the paint off the walls of the vacant building, then keyed in his password to retrieve the message.

"Hey, Will. This is Rick." He held the phone away from his ear and stared at the screen as Brent's voice droned on. What the fuck? Had he lost his ever-loving mind? He brought the device back up, catching the tail end of the message. "…need you to come to my place ASAP and take her off my hands. I gotta go to work soon."

Take her off his hands? What the fuck was he talking about? He hit the Replay button and closed his eyes, as he focused on every syllable. "Hey, Will. This is Rick. I've got an unexpected visitor. Lady says she needs to talk to you. I…" He could hear another voice in the background, female, most likely, but her words were unintelligible. Then Brent's voice returned, sounding muffled, like he'd pulled the phone away from his mouth. "I won't say anything. I know. You can put that thing down. I promise I won't say anything." Then more clearly, "I need you to come to my place, ASAP and take her off my hands. I gotta go to work soon."

Brent was a lot of things, but an actor he was not. Judging from the tremor in his voice, and the fact he'd been pretending to be *him*, calling *Will*, told him something was terribly wrong at his house. He dropped his tool belt where he stood, and as he took the stairs down to what would eventually be Sunny's new gallery, he placed a call to his oldest brother.

"Jake. We've got a problem." He relayed the bizarre message Brent had left. "Could it be Jessica?"

"Could be. Don't go in guns blazing." His brother knew him well. He kept a shotgun under the seat of his truck and a handgun attached to the underside of the dashboard via a heavy-duty magnet. Just in case. There were several other firearms stashed around the house, but they wouldn't do Brent any good since he didn't know about them. "I'll call a friend of mine on the police force. Wait for backup, Rick. If it is Jessica, she's batshit crazy."

He'd make no promises about waiting for backup. If Will's crazy ex was holding Brent at gunpoint, he wasn't going to sit on his hands and wait to see what she'd do when Will didn't show up. "Do not call Will. Keep him out of this."

Jake didn't make any promises, either, as he warned Rick again to wait for the police then hung up to make his call. Rick's truck was parked behind the store. Before getting in, he reached under the dashboard and released the Sig Sauer P226 from its hiding place. In a move he'd done thousands of times, he released the magazine, verified it was full, and shoved it back in before racking the slide to drop a round into the chamber. A quick look under the seat assured him the Henry 410 shotgun was still there. He hoped to hell he didn't need it.

As he turned the corner onto his street, he saw a familiar figure running down the walk. He pulled over and shoved the passenger side door open. "Get the fuck in here before she sees you, asshole."

His brother grabbed the door and hopped in, dragging ragged breaths in. "Is it Jessica?"

"You tell me." He pulled his phone out of his pocket. "Listen to my voicemail. See if you can identify her voice in the background."

He played the message on speaker. Brent's shaky voice was like a spear to his gut. He'd never forgive himself if something happened to him. The last time he'd spoken to the man was seconds before he'd taken his dick to the back of his throat. A lot of shit had gone down since then. Shit they needed to discuss. Shit Rick needed to apologize for. No way was he going to sit on his ass and let some crazy fucker take him away. Not on his watch.

"That's her." Will pointed to the phone. "That's Jessica." He braced an elbow on the passenger door and rubbed his upturned hand over his face. "What the fuck is she doing here?"

"Don't know. Don't care. But that's my guy in there. I'm not going to let her hurt him." He held the Sig close to his thigh. "You understand?"

"I understand." A muscle ticked in Will's jaw. "Let me go in and talk to her. See what she wants."

"Hell, no. I'm not letting you anywhere near her."

His brother faced him, his eyes burning with determination. "That's not for you to decide, asswipe. She's here because of me. I'll talk to her. Get her to let Brent out of there then I'll find out what she wants."

"No." He couldn't say it any plainer. "I spent eight fucking years busting down doors for a living. I can take her out."

"I know you can, but let me try talking to her first. It's me she wants, not Brent, or you, since she thinks he's you."

"She's armed," he reminded his brother. "You heard Brent. She's got a knife or a gun. She came here to kill you, bro. I'm not letting that happen."

"She won't kill me."

"What makes you so certain?"

"Because I'm going to buy you and the cops time to get in a position to stop her. If I don't show up soon, she'll get impatient, and she might harm Brent in retaliation. Remember, she thinks he has me in his phone contacts. She doesn't need him to get to me now."

The fucker was right. Who knew how long she'd wait for Will to respond to the voicemail Brent had left? His phone was the connection she needed. She might not kill Brent, but she could make him suffer as a means to encourage Will to meet with her. "Okay, but don't get anywhere near her. You hear me? Or I'll kill you myself when this is over."

His brother nodded. "I won't get close to her."

"If she has a handgun, you don't need to be close for her to make a lucky shot, but the farther you are away, the less accurate the firearm will be."

"Got it. Anything else?"

"Tell her you won't talk in front of me. Get Brent out of there then keep her talking. Provided she wants to talk. She might just want to kill you, so don't be a putz. Once Brent is out of there, try to get her to put her weapon down as a condition of talking."

"Is that all?"

"You got your phone on you?"

"Yeah. Why?"

"Put everything on silent then call me."

Will changed his phone sound settings to silent then placed a call to Rick.

He answered, put his phone on Mute, then instructed his brother to put his phone back in his pocket. "I'll be able to hear everything, I hope."

Will nodded.

"Okay. Let's do this."

Rick eased the pickup to the curb one house down from his and killed the engine. Before his brother stepped out, he cautioned him one more time. "Be careful, and if she starts shooting, run like hell."

Will raised an eyebrow. "Is that what the Marines do?"

"Fuck, no. But you aren't a Marine."

"Gotcha. I'll be careful. I know her. Or I did. She might be here to kill me, but she won't do it before she gives me an earful. If I'm right, I'm about to find out why she stole from me. I've always wondered. It never made any sense." He opened the door and put one foot on the ground. Halfway across the neighbor's lawn, he stopped and turned to face Rick who was still in the truck. "Nod if you can hear me."

Rick nodded.

"I'll try to get your boyfriend out in one piece, but in case things go wrong in there, I love you, bro. Tell Jake and Kenzie I love them, too."

Rick nodded.

Will resumed his casual stroll across the lawn as if there weren't a lunatic waiting for him. He didn't know if his brother was crazy or brave. Probably a little of both. He'd met Marines who would balk at walking into a situation like this with little to no backup.

He waited until Will let himself in the front door then he slipped out of the cab and made his way to the side of the house, stepping carefully to avoid alerting the intruder to his presence.

CHAPTER TWENTY-TWO

Will rapped his knuckles on Rick's front door, something he'd never do under normal circumstances, then turned the handle. The door opened on silent hinges, thanks to Rick's excellent maintenance of the aging abode. He poked his head inside. Seeing no one in the living room, he called out, "Rick! Hey, man. What's going on?" as he stepped inside like nothing was wrong. "Where the fuck are you?"

"In here." Brent's voice shook, but he was alive. He hoped Rick heard that. If it had been Kenzie in the same situation, he'd be a basket case, wondering if she was okay. Rick tried to play off his relationship with Brent as no big deal, but he'd seen more than Rick thought he had the morning he'd walked in on them. He'd seen enough to know the two men had feelings for each other. Feelings that found expression through a physical connection. Rick could protest all he wanted, but Brent wasn't a meaningless hookup. Which meant Will had to do whatever it took to keep the man safe. He'd never be able to look his brother in the eye again if he let his past interfere with Rick's future.

He crossed the room to the door leading to the tiny, eat-in kitchen. He paused in the doorway, taking in the scene. His former fiancée stood near the sink, a small revolver in her hand which she had pointed at Brent, who sat at the table, his face pale, his eyes wide behind his designer glasses. "You okay, Rick?"

His brother's boyfriend nodded which wouldn't do. Will had waited a long time to find out why Jessica had made off with his paintings and his money. The last thing he needed was Rick barreling in here, guns blazing, before he had a chance to talk to her. "Why don't you run along then, bro? Jessica and I need to talk." He cocked his head toward the door leading to the backyard. "Go on. This is none of your business."

Brent placed his hands on the table to leverage himself up. "Sit your ass back down." Jessica stepped closer, pressing the muzzle of the gun to his temple. Brent, trembling like a leaf in the wind, dropped his butt back to the chair.

"Okay. Okay. I'm not going anywhere."

"You can put the gun down, Jess. At least point it at me. I'm the one you came here for, not my brother."

"Don't flatter yourself, asshole." Jessica spat the words out. "You'd rather die than watch your brother die, so don't think I'll make this easy on you."

Shit. He hadn't known her at all, but apparently, she knew him too well. Rick's reminder to stall, rang in his ears. If he was going to get anything out of her, now was the time. "What do you want, Jess? You took everything I had. Left me practically destitute. Why'd you do that anyway? I thought we had a good life. I was painting the commercial crap you wanted me to paint."

Her lips twisted in a sinister sneer. "I see you're still the arrogant prick you were when we first met." That stung, but he kept his thoughts from showing on his face. "You were a means to an end, asshole."

"To what end? Prison?"

"Fuck you!" She turned the pistol on him. Hands raised, palms out, he took a step back. "If everything had gone as planned, you'd be dead by now and I'd be a fucking millionaire."

I'd be dead? What. The. Fuck? "You were going to kill me?"

"I sure as hell wasn't going to spend the rest of my life married to you."

"I don't understand." Truer words had never been spoken.

"Of course you don't. You never did see anything but the canvas in front of you. People didn't exist in your world unless they were there to satisfy your needs. You never gave a fuck about anyone but yourself." She waved the pistol toward Brent. "And your idiot brothers. You deserved everything I had planned for you."

The shit of it was, he couldn't argue with her. She'd nailed him. He'd always been more focused on his art than on the world around him. Achieving a measure of success had only made him narrow his focus more in an effort to propel his career forward. He'd seen Jessica as a tool he needed in his box to help him. It had taken her betrayal to open his eyes to his personal failings, and MacKenzie's love to show him what a relationship was supposed to look like. In a twisted sort of way, he owed Jessica for the life he had now. For the future he had with Kenzie. "What, exactly, did you have planned? I kind of thought you'd done enough."

"God, you didn't learn anything, did you?"

He'd learned plenty, but she didn't need to know that. "Guess not."

"I should have killed you when I had the chance, just on principal, but Cecil and Ginger told me to wait."

Does she know Ginger Carpenter is really Samantha Sheldon, Sunny's half-sister? It didn't seem like she knew, and he damn sure wasn't going to be the one to tell her. "Wait for what?"

"God, you are dense, aren't you?" She shifted so she faced him head-on. "I was supposed to wait until we were married, you idiot. As your grieving widow, I'd inherit the missing paintings."

"Which weren't missing because you knew where they were."

"Did that light bulb just flash on in your pea brain?"

"No. Ginger tried to frame Sunny Sheldon for the theft, but she screwed up and got caught. I got all my paintings back."

"Another pea brain." She shook her head. "Her and Cecil both."

"So, let me get this straight." His brother had granted him the opportunity to get the answers he wanted, but he wasn't stupid enough to think Rick was going to stand around twiddling his thumbs, hoping the she-bitch was going to let her hostages go. Keeping her talking would allow Rick and the cops time to get in place. "You were going to marry me. Then you were going to kill me. After my death, the stolen paintings would miraculously be found, and because they'd gone up in value following my death, you'd sell them and make millions. Do I have that right?"

"It was a sound plan."

"Only we didn't get married."

"You wouldn't set the date! I kept nagging you to, but you had your head in your paintings!"

Thank god he had. At least one good thing came out of his tunnel vision. MacKenzie would get a kick out of that since he was still guilty of getting lost in his work at times. He made a mental note to set a wedding date—the sooner, the better—if Jessica didn't kill him first.

"So you just decided to rob me blind instead?"

"That was Cecil's decision. He let that airhead actress of his convince him to go ahead with the plan, sans the wedding and killing you. We'd have to hold on to the paintings a lot longer, but we were eventually going to sell them on the black market. We still would have made a fortune, but that bimbo pushed her own agenda and got caught."

He'd thought he'd lost everything when he'd raised his head up long enough to realize Jess was gone and she'd taken everything with her, but in reality, she'd done him a solid. The least he could do was return the favor. "Jess, give me the gun." He held his hand out, palm up. "If you don't, you aren't going to get out of here alive."

"You're the one who's going to die, asshole. You think I came all this way to reminisce?"

"No, I think you came here to kill me, but that isn't going to happen. If you try, they'll kill you."

"Who? What are you talking about?"

She'd been so focused on telling her story and berating him, she'd failed to see the officer signaling him through the kitchen window. "The house is surrounded, Jess. At the very least, let this guy go. He's not my brother."

Her eyes widened. "What? Who the hell is he?"

"Just a guy who rents a room from Rick. No one important. He's certainly not worth the death penalty."

"You're lying."

He shook his head. "No, I'm not." He glanced at Brent. "Tell her who you are."

His brother's boyfriend opened his mouth. Closed it then tried again. "My name is Brent. I'm not related to Will or Rick in any way."

"See? I didn't lie about him, and I'm not lying about the house being surrounded." He raised his voice. "Rick! Show her that big-ass gun you have in your hands."

The barrel of a gun came into sight in the window.

"Jess, look." He nodded toward the window. "Rick's a Marine. He won't miss, and even if he did, the entire Willowbrook PD is out there now. You might get off a shot. Maybe two, before someone takes you out. Think about it, Jess. So far, you're only charged with theft, and since I got all the paintings and my money back, I'm willing to put in a good word for you. But you have to let Brent go, and give me the gun."

She glanced at the window then her gaze darted to Brent then him. She chewed on her bottom lip, a habit he recalled her doing when she was trying to work something out in her mind. He'd thought it cute, once upon a time. Not so much when he knew she was contemplating who to kill first, him or Brent. "Stop this before you get in so deep you can't get out, Jess."

"Did you ever love me? Even just a little?"

Her questions, asked with a little bit of a pout in her voice, cut him to the quick. He'd come to terms with the shitty way he'd treated her, and he understood how his actions had played a part in what she and the others had done to him. He'd hurt her, and she'd hurt him right back.

"I did," he lied. Now that he knew what real love felt like, he could see he'd never loved Jessica, not in the way she meant. This wasn't the time to confess that, either. "I was devastated when you left me." That much was true, though he'd mourned the loss of his paintings and his cash more than he'd missed her. Another thing she didn't need to know.

Her lips lifted in a weak smile, and her gaze softened. Thinking he'd convinced her, he held out his hand for the gun. She swayed toward him then she blinked, twice. A grimace replaced the smile on her face, and her gaze hardened. Another blink, and Will's heart vaulted to his throat as she lifted her arm and pointed the gun at his chest.

~ ~ ~

Considering he had more experience facing off with armed gunmen than all three of Willowbrook's police officers combined, it didn't take much to convince them to let him enter the house while they waited outside both exits, in case Jessica decided to make a run for it.

Rick eased the window in Brent's room open and crawled through. Lowering himself to the floor, Sig in hand, he belly-crawled to the door and down the short hallway to the kitchen. Rick had swapped phones with the senior officer in charge so they could listen in on Will's conversation while he got closer. With his front-row seat, he could hear everything being said, and it made his blood run cold. The bitch had planned to murder his brother in order to drive up the prices of the missing paintings that would mysteriously be found in Sunny's gallery after his death. Will's tunnel vision when it came to his work had saved his life.

As his brother kept his former fiancée talking, Rick eased the camera aperture on the borrowed phone past the doorframe until he had a visual on what was going on in the kitchen. Rick stood with his back to the interior door. Jessica, gun in her unsteady hand, stood with her back to the window above the sink. He adjusted the camera angle, caught a glimpse of Brent sitting at the table. Still wearing the clothes he'd worn to Jake's party the previous evening; a day's worth of stubble roughened his clenched jaw. Under normal circumstances, Rick would have thought the look to be sexy as hell, but closer examination revealed bags beneath terror-filled eyes. *Hang in there, baby. I'll get you out of there.*

He forced his attention away from Brent and onto the woman who had put that look in his lover's eyes. With every word out of Jessica's mouth, he mentally charted her downward spiral. She'd come with an agenda, and Will's trip down memory lane was only serving to reinforce the fucked-up reasons she'd come up with this plan in the first place. She'd meant to kill him before, and cheated of that opportunity, she wasn't about to let another get away. With no way to communicate his thoughts to his brother, he had no choice but to stand by and let the situation unfold and hope to hell his reflexes were still quick enough to react once she lost her shit. Because he had no doubt she was going to. Her intent was in her erratic gestures and every quavering word from her lips.

"Stop this before you get in so deep you can't get out, Jess."

Keep her talking, Will.

"Did you ever love me? Even just a little?"

Shit. Judging by the way her voice wavered, things were quickly going to hell in a handbasket. He adjusted his grip on the only weapon he'd brought with him, the 9mm Sig, and prepared to do whatever needed to be done to protect the people he loved.

His heart tripped over itself. *The people I love.* No question, he loved his brother, would do anything for him, but Brent? Taking a deep breath in through his nose, he let the thought of loving Brent settle. *Do I love him?* He winced recalling the tight band around his chest and the pain of betrayal when Brent had arrived at Jake's party with another man. Seeing Brent's bravery in the face of a madwoman made him face the truth his heart had known for some time. *I love him. I really fucking love him.* And there wasn't anything he wouldn't do for the people he loved.

"I did," Will told her. "I was devastated when you left me."

Rick didn't know if Will had ever really loved Jessica, but he wasn't lying about the devastation she'd left in her wake. His brother had been a shell of a man when he'd returned home to Willowbrook. It had taken him months, and the love of a good woman, to come out of the funk he'd been in. Rick had been as bad as Will when he'd come home. Renovating the house he'd grown up in and starting his own construction business had gone a long way to lifting him out of his own personal pit of self-pity, but Brent had stolen his heart and given him a reason to want to live.

I love him. God, how I love him.

He forced himself to concentrate on the gun-wielding woman standing in his kitchen. Her lips lifted in a weak smile, and her gaze softened.

Ask her for the gun, bro. Ask her now.

As if he'd heard Rick's thoughts, his brother extended his hand—a silent invitation for her to hand the weapon over.

Do it. Do it. Do it.

She swayed toward his brother, blinked twice, then her pseudo-smile turned to a grimace and her gaze hardened. Another blink.

Oh shit.

Rick dropped the phone and stepped into the open doorway, drawing the woman's attention away from her two hostages. Time slowed as it had many times when he'd been in the middle of a firefight.

Jessica raised her arm.

Will dove.

Rick stared down the barrel of her gun.

Two shots rang out simultaneously, deafening in the confined space.

A searing pain in his abdomen doubled him over.

He raised his weapon and fired again as Will tackled the assailant to the floor.

Another shot rent the air. More pain, this time in his right shoulder. He dropped to his knees.

Eight fucking years with the Marines, been in more gun battles than I can count, and I get shot in my own home.

I love you, Brent.

His world faded to black.

CHAPTER TWENTY-THREE

Silence. Deafening silence followed the split second of terror-inducing, ear-splitting, gunfire. Beneath the table where he'd taken cover the second the crazy woman had pointed her gun at Will, Brent slowly uncoiled. Nearby, Will lay motionless atop their assailant. The gun she'd pointed at him lay on the floor near her limp hand. Blood was everywhere. On the floor. The chair he'd been sitting in. Splattered on the legs of the table. Bile rose in his throat, but he swallowed it back down.

Will. He had to help him. *Oh god! The man in the doorway!* The one he'd caught the barest glimpse of as he dove beneath the table. He swung his gaze away from Will. All he could see of the man was from the thighs down, but it was enough. *Rick.* Will hadn't lied to the woman. *Rick is here!* Had come to save them.

Tears of gratitude and love welled in his eyes. On his hands and knees, he crawled out of his hiding place when Rick's knees bent. And the man who owned his heart crashed to the floor, terror like nothing he'd ever known in his life seized him.

"Rick!" He scrambled, pushing empty chairs aside in a desperate attempt to get to the man's side. "Rick! Somebody! Help!" He felt, more than heard, heavy footsteps approaching, seemingly from every direction as he knelt beside the inert figure. "Rick!" he wailed. "Rick!"

"Brent. Brent!" A firm hand on his shoulder. He looked up and met Will's gaze. "You gotta move, man. Let the EMTs take over."

EMTs? A trio of uniformed men and a woman loaded down with equipment bags crowded the hallway. Reining in his fear, he allowed Will to help him to his feet, giving the team room to work. The first of the bunch brushed past them. Brent followed his progress and was stunned to see the small room filled with police.

"Pulse is weak." The comment drew his attention to the paramedic attending to Rick. "Let's roll him over and see what we've got."

"Come on." Will wrapped a hand around the back of Brent's neck and pulled him face-first into his chest and held him there while Brent bawled his eyes out. "He's going to be okay. He won't leave us like this."

"He saved us." He hiccupped the words out.

Will stroked the back of his head. "He's a hero. Got a chest full of medals hidden under his bed. It'll take more than this to take him away from us."

"We're going to transport him now." The woman's voice over his shoulder had him pulling out of Will's embrace. "We've got a chopper waiting at the football field to take him to a trauma unit in Dallas." She named the hospital.

"We'll follow." He pointed to one of the officers occupying the kitchen. "Steve has my phone number. Call if there's any news?"

The woman nodded. Behind her, the three men she'd come in with lifted Rick's still body to a gurney and strapped him in. "I'll get the info from Steve. Drive safe. He'll need you when he wakes up."

It was Will's turn to nod then he took Brent's hand in his and they followed the team out the door. They were on the lawn, watching them load Rick into the ambulance when Jake ran up the street. "What the hell happened?"

Will faced his brother. "The bitch shot him. Twice, I think."

His boss's face turned white. "Sonofabitch. I'm going to kill her with my bare hands."

"Not necessary." Will shook his head. "Rick beat you to it."

"She's dead?"

"Yeah." Will held up his hands. Brent shivered at the dried blood in the creases of his knuckles and rimming his fingernails. "He saved our lives."

"Fucking hero," Jake muttered. He dragged Will into a hug. "You okay?"

"Fine."

Jake let Will go then pulled Brent in for a hug. "You okay?"

"Physically, yeah."

His boss drew back and, hands on Brent's shoulders, looked him over. "Have a little faith in him, Brent. He's going to be okay."

"You don't know that."

"Yes, I do." He glanced at Will then to Brent. "Because we won't let him be anything else."

Will nodded. "They're life-flighting him to Dallas. We need to go."

"My car's down the street." Jake took off at a brisk clip. Brent fell into step with Will as they followed the oldest Ingram brother to where he'd left his car.

He'd made the long drive to and from Dallas more times than he wanted to think about. Jake had a steady hand on the wheel and a heavy foot on the gas pedal, but still, the miles crept by as Brent stared, unseeing, at the passing scenery. He tried closing his eyes, but that only made the images burned onto his brain more vivid. For as long as he lived, he'd never forget Rick laying lifeless on the floor or the scent of blood permeating the air.

Rick had saved his and Will's lives. If he hadn't been there, Jessica would have killed Will then, he had no doubt, she would have turned the gun on him. He'd seen the desperation in her eyes when she'd confronted him in the kitchen. He still wasn't sure exactly what she'd done to Rick's brother in the past, only what he'd spoken of to try to talk her off the ledge, and he didn't care. She was, make that *had been*, off her rocker.

"You okay back there?"

He met Jake's gaze in the rearview mirror. "Can you drive any faster?"

"I could," his boss replied. "But Rick's going to need us to be all in one piece to help him recover."

Not trusting his voice, Brent nodded.

Will glanced over his shoulder. "He's going to be okay. The two of you will have a lifetime together."

Guilt was a lead weight anchoring his heart to his toes. He hoped Will was right, but he'd fucked up, big-time. The moment he'd spotted Kenn sitting on the front porch, he should have called a car service to pick him up and return him to whatever hole he'd crawled out of. Instead, he'd taken him to Jake's party just to spite Rick.

Fresh tears pricked his eyes. Facing the window, he swiped at them with the palm of his hand. He'd been an ass to Rick, and the man had still come to his rescue. He'd taken a bullet, maybe two.

He sucked in a deep breath. "I don't deserve your brother."

"What's that you say?" Will gave him the stink-eye over the seat.

"It's true. I don't deserve him."

"Did you fuck that guy you were with last night?" Jake's glare in the mirror matched Will's tight inquiry.

Brent shook his head then focused on the old-fashioned map book peeking out of the seat back pocket. "No, but I used him to make Rick jealous, so I might as well have. The result's the same."

"How do you figure?" Being on the receiving end of Jake's questioning reminded Brent why the man was such a good lawyer. He could slice a witness in half with his voice alone.

"He sent my call to voicemail this morning. I'm surprised he listened to the message I left." He dropped his voice to a whisper. "He had no reason to."

"Bringing that guy to the party was a shitty thing to do. Rick hid it well, but he was hurt."

Brent glanced at the back of Will's head. "I shouldn't have done it. I regretted it as soon as we got there. I should have stayed away, like Rick wanted me to."

"What?" Jake glanced over his shoulder then focused on the road ahead. "Rick didn't want you there?"

"He didn't. Rick sent me a text earlier saying he would be working late and not to expect him home for dinner. I only knew about the party because Jean mentioned she'd see me there. I put two and two together. He didn't want to be seen with me."

"That's bullshit." Will shook his head.

Jake spoke to his brother. "He told me Brent was working late."

"Yeah. He told me something like that, too," Will confirmed.

After that, they made the rest of the trip in silence. By the time they'd parked and found out Rick was in surgery, Brent had made up his mind. He couldn't stay in Willowbrook. Couldn't work for Rick's brother and live in his house any longer.

They'd been in the designated waiting room for less than half an hour when Sunny and MacKenzie arrived. Brent's heart ached as he sat alone, watching as whispered words and hugs were exchanged. He recalled the way Will had embraced him at the house. The way his strong arms had reminded him so much of his brother's. Unable to sit and watch, he walked away. Surely, there had to be a drink machine somewhere.

A kind nurse pointed him toward the cafeteria where he purchased a cup of tea and found a seat in a back corner, away from prying eyes. He didn't know how long he sat there, but by the time he wandered into the waiting room, it was filled with people he recognized from Willowbrook.

Jake pushed his way through the crowd. "Where the fuck have you been? We've been looking all over for you!"

"I went to the cafeteria. Why? Is Rick out of surgery?"

"Over an hour ago. He's in recovery, and they said the only person he wants to see is you."

His heart lodged in his throat. "Me?" he croaked.

"Told you so." Will joined them, clapping Brent on the back. "My brother's crazy about you."

Ignoring Will's optimism, he asked, "He's going to be okay?"

Jake ran a hand through his hair. "Doctor said he's got a long road ahead, but he's going to be okay. Go see him. They'll only let one person at a time in, so let him see your face then come out so we can have a chance at him."

Will put a hand on his brother's chest. "Jake's going to rip him a new one for getting himself shot then he's probably going to finish the job Jessica started." He was all smiles as he said it, but from the look on Jake's face, it wasn't far from the truth. They'd almost lost their brother today. Hero or not, Jake wasn't going to let it rest.

"Are you sure?" Brent massaged his nape. "Family should probably go first."

Jake pinned him with a look. "I would have been in there an hour ago, but the doc said Rick wanted you and nobody else. The fucker."

"So go, would you?" Will shoved him toward the door. "Apologize or whatever it is you need to do to make him happy. There are a lot of people out here who want to see him."

"You must be Brent." A nurse greeted him at the door leading to the recovery wing.

"Yes, ma'am. I'm here to see Rick Ingram."

She gave him a bright smile. "Thank god you're here. Mr. Ingram has asked about you every few minutes. I thought we were going to have to put out an APB to locate you."

"I'm sorry. I went to the cafeteria, and I guess the time got away from me."

She stopped in front of a closed door. "No worries. You're here now. Just let me peek inside to make sure he's awake. Don't stay too long. He needs his rest, and I'm sure there are other family members anxious to see him."

"I'm sorry if they've been giving you a hard time."

"We're used to it, but I have to say, his brothers have been persistent."

"I won't stay long. They told me Rick's only allowed one visitor at a time, but it might be in everyone's best interest if you let both his brothers in together. Jake's a little worked up right now."

She held his gaze while she digested what he was saying. "I'll take your recommendation under advisement." Then she pushed the door open just enough to peek in.

Rick's voice bellowed through the crack. "Did you fucking find him yet?"

The nurse, Karen, her badge said, glanced back at Brent. "He's all yours." She pushed the door wide.

"It's about fucking time!" Rick grimaced as he tried to shift his weight. "Where the hell have you been?"

Needing a moment to collect himself, Brent focused his gaze on Nurse Karen. "Thank you."

"You're welcome." She winked at him. "See if you can get him to calm down."

"I'll do my best." The door shut behind him, leaving them alone. "You wanted to see me?"

"Where the fuck were you?"

"The cafeteria. Their tea sucks, by the way."

CHAPTER TWENTY-FOUR

Rick had never been so happy to see anyone in his entire life as he was to see Brent standing there, hale and hearty. Not a scratch on him. Nurse Karen told him both his brothers were in the waiting room, and, according to her, "in perfect health and mad as hornets" over his refusal to see them. The fuckers could wait. No one had been able or willing to tell him where Brent had disappeared to, and, in his mind, that meant they were keeping something from him. Had he screwed up? Had the bitch shot Brent? He wasn't going to quit until he knew for certain, one way or the other. Now that he knew Brent was safe, anger, at himself, replaced the fear he'd been living with since he'd woken up in the hospital.

He'd been such a fucking fool. This morning was a reminder of how short life could be, and he'd wasted enough of his hiding who he was and denying himself happiness because he worried about what other people would think. Fuck them. He didn't give a shit what anyone thought anymore. No one, except Brent. He blew out a cleansing breath. "I'm sorry, baby. I should have been there when you got home this morning."

Brent sniffed. "It's okay. I should have come home last night. I deliberately waited until I knew you'd be at work before I came home this morning." His lover dissolved into a puddle of tears. "This is all my fault," he wailed.

He had a lot to say to the man, and he wasn't going to do it from across the room. His right arm was in a sling, so he wiggled the fingers of his left hand. "Come here." When Brent didn't budge, he dropped his voice an octave. "Come here, Brent. I need to fucking touch you."

Brent swiped at the tears tracking down his cheeks as he shuffled to the bedside. Rick reached for his hand. His skin was warm and reassuring. He hadn't realized what he had until he'd almost lost it. "Never should have let you leave the house yesterday. I'm fucking never letting you out of my sight again."

The lawyer sobbed harder, if that was possible.

"When they wouldn't tell me where you were, I thought the bitch had shot you or something, and they didn't want to tell me. Christ, I was going out of my mind, worrying about you."

His gorgeous lips formed a shocked O. "They didn't tell you I rode here with Jake and Will?"

"They did, but when they didn't or wouldn't say where you were, I thought they were lying to me."

Brent shook his head. "I'm so sorry. I just needed some time to myself to think. I wandered around the hospital for a while then some nurse pointed me to the cafeteria. That place is creepy. Lots of dark corners."

"You were in one of them?"

He nodded.

"What were you thinking about?"

Brent sucked in a shaky breath then let it out. "You. Me. Us."

"I've been thinking about us, too." The events of the previous day were branded on his memory as some of the worst moments of his life. Getting caught with his dick down another man's throat wasn't the way he'd pictured his brothers finding out he was gay, but that was the way it happened, and he hadn't dealt with it well. He stroked the back of Brent's hand with his thumb. "I can't apologize enough for yesterday, baby. I wanted to stop you from leaving the house so bad, but I was afraid you'd tell me no."

Brent squeezed his fingers. "I wanted to stay, to let you know I wasn't ashamed of what we were doing, but that moment belonged to you. You needed to deal with your brother on your own terms." He let out a long sigh, his gaze focused on something across the room. "It hurt to walk out the door and leave you there, and I'll admit, it hurt worse that you let me. I thought you were ashamed to admit you had feelings for me."

Rick dropped his head to the pillow and groaned. "I'm so fucking sorry. I don't want you to ever feel that way again." He raised his head. "Look at me." When Brent's gaze locked with his, he said the words he'd never said to anyone other than his brothers. "I love you. I'm not ashamed to admit that, and I'm not ashamed I want you more than I've ever wanted anyone in my life. I'm a stupid fuck for letting you think for a minute you don't mean the world to me, but if you'll give me another chance, I promise I'll make it up to you. I'll never let you out of my sight again."

Brent squeezed his hand, giving him courage "I understand if you don't want to be with me." His voice sounded like he'd gargled with gravel as he brought up the subject that had left a hole in his heart. "The guy you were with last night. He means something to you?"

He wasn't sure if the sound Brent made was a laugh or a cry. "He's nothing, Rick. Nothing at all."

God, it hurt to say the words. "But you spent the night with him."

"No. I dropped him off at a hotel and got myself a room at a different hotel." Brent flipped their linked hands over, caressing the back of Rick's with his thumb. "Kenn's my ex. I asked him to move to Willowbrook with me, but he declined. He was sitting on our porch when I got home from work yesterday. He said all the right things, but seeing him, I realized he wasn't what I wanted anymore."

"When I saw the two of you together, I don't know who I wanted to murder more, you or him."

"I'm so sorry. I was hurt and pissed at you for what happened that morning. Jean spilled the beans about the party, and that pissed me off even more. Kenn was spouting off about wanting to give Willowbrook a chance, so I figured I could kill two birds with one stone. I'd show you I didn't need you and get Kenn off my back at the same time."

"Did it work? Did you get him off your back?"

Brent smiled. "Is that what you picked up on?"

"Yeah." He grinned. "Sue me, lawyer. I *know* you need me, so tell me the fucker isn't coming back."

His gaze was tender, his voice soft. "He's not, Rick. And if he did, I'd tell him the same thing I told him last night."

The beeping of his heart monitor took off like a racehorse out of the chute. Nurse Brenda would be rushing in any second now to see what the heck was going on. "What's that?"

"That I've given my heart to someone else." He brought Rick's hand up to his lips and placed a kiss on his knuckles. "I hope he doesn't crush it."

"I won't." Christ, he was going to cry. Maybe it was the pain meds. It *had to be* the pain meds. "I won't, Brent. I promise." He inhaled a ragged breath. Shit, it even hurt to breathe. "I thought I was in love once, and when he left, it nearly killed me. But what I felt for him was nothing compared to what I feel for you. I love you, and it took seeing you held at gunpoint to get me to admit it. For a second there, I thought I might not get the chance to tell you."

"The night I put your drunk ass to bed…"

Rick forced a smile to his lips. "I bare my heart to you, and *that's* what you ask about?"

"Yeah. Tell me, baby. I want to know everything about you."

He nodded. "We'd been together for six years." The words came easier than he'd imagined they would. He told Brent everything, from the way he'd met Dave to the fucked-up way their relationship had ended. "I thought he was the love of my life. I was wrong. If we'd loved each other enough, we would have done anything to be together. He wasn't willing to come out of the closet for me, and I wasn't willing to come out for him."

"Would you have come out for me if Will hadn't walked in on us?"

"Truth?"

Brent nodded.

"Not right away, but I would have, eventually. I was already thinking about telling my brothers, but what happened this morning made me realize how short life is, and that I don't want to waste another minute pretending *you* aren't my life."

He shook his head. "I understand Will came out of this unscathed. I should kill him for putting you in danger."

"It wasn't his fault. I heard everything she said. She was deranged. Probably has been for a long time but hid it well. He was taken in by her, so don't blame him."

His brother had admitted as much when they'd talked about his time in New York, but if he'd never gotten involved with the woman in the first place, none of this would have happened.

"Besides, if she hadn't shown up here, who knows how long it would have taken you to see the error of your ways."

Grinning, Rick shook his head. "Fuck off, asshole."

"Hmm. Sounds like a plan, dickwad."

Rick squeezed his hand. "You like my dick."

"I do. Very much." His gaze smoldered. "You know what else I like?"

Breathless, his heart tripping all over itself again, he asked, "What?"

"Your lips. I need to feel them on me. Can I kiss you?"

"If you don't, I'm going to get out of this bed and kick your ass."

Brent's smile was pure evil as he bent, bringing his lips to within an inch of where Rick wanted them to be. His breath brushed Rick's cheek, his comment for Rick's ears only. "There are lots of things I want you to do to my ass. Kicking isn't one of them." Then he stole the breath from his lungs with a kiss that promised more carnal things to come. He didn't know how long they kissed before a familiar voice interrupted them.

"Jesus, Brent," Jake said. "At least wait until he's had a chance to recover before you molest him."

They both groaned. Gazes locked; Brent placed one last peck on his lips then straightened to face his boss. "I thought they said only one visitor at a time."

Jake looked worse than a mile of bad road. His hair stood on end, his skin was pale, and his face had acquired a whole new set of deeply etched lines. "They did, but you were taking so fucking long, I threatened to sue them if they didn't let me see my brother."

Rick smiled. "Throwing your weight around, big brother?"

"Just wanted to see for myself that you were going to be okay." His voice was thick with emotion. "It's not every day one of my brothers gets shot in his own home." He cleared his throat. "How are you feeling?"

"Better, now that Brent's here." He tried to shift to a more comfortable position but every time he moved, it felt like someone stabbed him with a white-hot poker. He clenched his jaw hard enough to break molars. No way was he letting Jake know how bad he hurt.

Jake nodded. "You look like shit. Don't know what he sees in you." He addressed both of them. "Sunny wants you both to stay at our house, at least until the police release the property. Right now, it's a crime scene. The investigation could take a while."

Rick had seen more than his share of crime scenes. He'd have to hire someone to clean the place. Even though he'd recently remodeled the kitchen, he'd probably want to do it all over again. Give it a fresh look to erase the bad memories associated with its present décor.

"It's an open invitation. You can stay with us as long as you want. We didn't know if you'd want to go back there anytime soon."

Brent squeezed his hand. "I appreciate the offer, Jake, and maybe we'll take you up on it when Rick is released, but for now, I'm planning on staying here."

"Jake makes a good point," Rick said. "Staying at his place, at least for a while, makes a lot of sense."

Jake's gaze darted between him and Brent then landed on Rick. "Nothing has to be decided today, so think about it, okay?" He cleared his throat again. "Sorry about the interruption, but now that I've seen you for myself, I can relax a little." His gaze swung to Brent. "Kenzie offered to go get coffee and snacks. Can we get anything for you?"

"Thanks, but I'm good."

Jake paused in the doorway. "The police want to talk to both of you. I told them I'd let them know when Rick was up to talking. As your lawyer, I'm advising both of you to not say anything to anyone about what happened unless I'm present. Understood?" They both nodded. "Okay, then."

The door closed behind him. *Thank god.* "Push that for me?" He pointed to the button the nurse had shown him earlier. If the pain got too bad, all he had to do was push it and he'd get another shot of the good stuff.

"You're hurting. I won't stay much longer. You need your rest."

"I'm fine. I could use a nap though." He reached for Brent's hand. "You really want to go back to our house? After everything that happened?"

"Your brother is a great boss, and Sunny is about the nicest person I've ever met."

"But?"

"It's one thing for my boss to know I'm fucking his brother. It's another for me to do it in his home."

Rick smiled so hard, it was a wonder his cheekbones didn't shatter. The meds were kicking in and he was drifting, so his smile might have looked a little goofy. Fuck, if he cared. All that mattered was that he hadn't lost Brent. "I gotcha. Our place it is." His head lolled on the pillow and his eyelids slid shut. He couldn't wait to take Brent home and start their life together.

EPILOGUE

Two years later…

What passed for the spring season in Texas was in full swing as Rick followed his brothers down the aisle between rows of white folding chairs set up on Jake's lawn. The sun would soon set on a picture-perfect day, the majesty of it framed by an arch covered in Texas wildflowers. Taking his place beneath the vibrant floral display, Rick faced away from the stunning show on the horizon and toward the brilliance of his future. In a few short minutes, he'd formally pledge his love and his life to the man who had taught him the meaning of love.

Brent had come into his life when Rick had been at his lowest. He'd left a career he loved on the faithless promises of another man and had his heart shattered. He'd found some peace in the business he'd created with a little help from his brothers, but it was Brent's love that had mended his heart. It was Brent who gave him the courage to own his truth and to live his truth.

Patience was a virtue he'd learned while in the Marines, and it served him well as he waited for his groom to make an appearance. He wasn't sure anyone would come, besides immediate family, but he should have known better. Every seat had been taken, and several members of the community stood along the back rows. Like every other event in Willowbrook, no invitation was needed. If you wanted to go, you went. Some, he knew, were there to witness a spectacle—a same-sex marriage—but most were there because they loved and supported one or both of the men pledging themselves today.

On his side, he acknowledged several people with a chin nod or a smile, or both. Cathy, who he'd dated in high school had been one of the first of his childhood friends to voice her support for his choice in life partners, claiming she'd suspected back then that he batted for the other team—her words, not his. If anyone would have suspected, it would have been her. He'd tried with her, but the depth of feeling she'd expected and the depth he'd been capable of had been two different things. In hindsight, he should have been more forthright with her. At the very least, he should have told her about his plan to enlist right after graduation. In his own defense, though, he hadn't told anyone. Not even his brothers and especially not his dad.

Several of his teachers were in attendance, and a bunch of kids he'd grown up with. He hadn't kept in touch with any of them while he was away, but in a small community like Willowbrook, it was hard to maintain any kind of distance. Over time, he'd run into one, then another, then another, until, slowly, he'd been pulled back into the social fabric of his small town. A few had turned their backs on him, but most had accepted Brent as his partner without question or censure. He shouldn't have kept his secret so long, but that was water under the proverbial bridge. He had Brent to thank for giving him the courage to live the life he deserved.

Speaking of…where the hell was he? He checked his watch, his gut clenching when he saw the time. Two minutes late. *What. The. Fuck?* He was going to kill him, right after he fucked him silly for making him wait.

Jake, his co-best man along with Will, leaned in. "He's coming. Nothing to worry about."

He wasn't worried, just pissed. He hated being the center of attention, and standing here with nearly everyone he knew wondering if he'd been stood up, made his skin crawl. Brent was going to pay for his tardiness but in a way they would both enjoy.

Returning his gaze to the crowd, he smiled at Jake's wife, Sunny, who bounced their baby girl, Amy, on her lap. Beside her, Will's wife, MacKenzie, cradled her baby bump with a loving hand as she winked at him. He winked back then his gaze briefly locked with that of his former lover, Dave Turner, who knew him well enough to crack a smile at his discomfort. The fucker. He'd shown up over a year ago, having left his fiancée at the altar. He said he hadn't expected Rick to pine away for him, and with Brent by his side, Rick had spent hours talking to Dave about the past and what they both wanted in the future. He'd told his fiancée the truth before leaving town, and with his and Brent's encouragement, he'd broken the news to his immediate family. They'd responded by cutting off all communication with him, so he'd moved into the apartment over Sunny's gallery and had rented another vacant storefront on Main Street and opened a gym that offered the usual fitness machines; plus, Dave acted as a personal trainer for those who needed a little extra push.

With a chin nod, Rick let his gaze wander to Brent's side of the aisle. He recognized several locals who were also Brent's clients at the law office. Then there was Jean and her husband who could have sat on either side of the aisle. Brent's large family had turned out for the occasion. All three of his younger sisters were seated in the front row. Aunts, uncles, and cousins filled up most of the next several rows. His dad and mom were to walk him down the aisle, preceded by his two brothers, who would stand up for him.

Shortly after he and Brent had officially announced they were a couple, they'd traveled to Houston to meet his family. To say he'd been surprised would be the understatement of the century. Brent had failed to mention his father was the commanding general of the largest Army base in Texas and that both his brothers were Army Rangers. Rick had nearly shit his pants when his father had answered the door in his full dress uniform. When they'd returned to their hotel room, Brent had paid for not warning him in advance.

After a smile and finger wave to Brent's sisters, his gaze wandered toward the rear of the seating arrangement where he found another face that had become familiar to him. Kenneth Westinghouse. The famous cartoonist, and Brent's former lover, sat on the back row. Kenn had been a pain in Rick's ass since the day they'd met, but once he'd made it clear Brent was his, and always would be, Kenn had come around. He'd recently moved to Dallas, partly to be closer to Brent, but mainly to get his life in order. He'd grown tired of the shallow party scene he'd been a part of in Houston and was looking for a deeper, more satisfying life now. Brent had plans to introduce their former lovers to each other at the reception later today. Rick wasn't sure it was a good idea, but they were grown men. They could decide for themselves.

Just as Kenn acknowledged him with a wide grin, movement near the pool house drew Rick's attention. Over the shoulders of the standing-room-only crowd, he caught a glimpse of a tan beret. Then another, advancing on his position. The hummingbirds in his stomach took flight, and his heart lodged in his throat as the men wearing the headgear drew closer.

It was hard to believe Brent and these men were related. His groom shared a lot of the same facial features, and he equaled them in height, but that was where the similarities ended. Brent kept in shape, but the two military men had the physique to go with their elite warrior status. Rick had worked with several Army Rangers overseas and had nothing but respect for the men who wore those berets.

The two men paused at the back of the makeshift aisle, allowing time for Brent and their parents to catch up. The moment the music began and his soon-to-be brothers-in-law stepped down the aisle, Rick got his first glimpse of his groom.

Flanked by his father, wearing his dress uniform, on one side, and his mother on the other, Brent looked like a million bucks in his tuxedo. Their gazes locked, and Rick's knees gave out. He was sinking like a rock, but before he hit the ground, strong arms lifted him to a standing position. Jake, the fucker, laughed in his left ear, while Brent's brother, Bryce, whispered, none to softly, "Stand the fuck up, Marine, before I whoop your ass."

Rick brushed both their well-meaning hands away. "I'm standing." He glared at Bryce who smirked at him before taking his place on the opposite side of the archway. They'd given him shit for being a Marine since the day they'd met, but it was all in fun…so they claimed. He wasn't so sure, but for the sake of familial peace, he held his tongue. What mattered was the way they supported their kid brother, and for that, Rick would take whatever shit they shoveled his way and do it with a smile on his face.

Jake elbowed him in the ribs. "Buck it up, brother. You're about to get hitched."

He jerked his attention away from Bryce. Brent and his parents had stopped two steps away. His mother broke ranks first, coming to place a kiss on Rick's cheek, whispering in his ear before she stepped back, "Take care of my baby."

Taking her hands in his, Rick nodded. "I will. I promise."

Brent's dad took her place, offering his hand. His grip was firm, as were his words of advice, given with the kind of smile he bet made hardened warriors piss their pants. "Hurt him and you'll wish you were never born."

Rick nodded, offering his truth in return for the man's honesty. "I used to wish that, sir, but your son gave me a reason to live. I won't hurt him. You have my word."

He patted their joined hands with his free one then released his hold. Brent's father acknowledged his other sons then he and his wife took the front row seats reserved for them. As soon as they were seated, Rick turned his gaze to the man he would spend the rest of his life with. Brent remained there, two steps away, his eyes shining with love and maybe an unshed tear or two. Rick held out his hand, palm up. When Brent took it, he closed his fingers and drew the man closer.

Before he and his brothers had left Jake's house to walk the hundred yards or so to the archway erected especially for his wedding, Will had asked if he was sure. He'd assured his brother that he was, but looking into Brent's eyes, he knew for certain. He'd been attracted to him from the first moment he'd laid eyes on him, but that was nothing compared to the overwhelming, all-encompassing, knee-weakening love he held for the man now.

He'd gotten to know the man behind the awesome body and nerd glasses and found him to have a heart of gold. He'd helped countless people in their small town and had been instrumental in encouraging acceptance for all. By some miracle, he'd looked at Rick and seen past the broken man he'd been on the night they met. He'd told Brent's father his son had given him a reason to live, but it was more than that. He'd taught him how to live.

~ ~ ~

Brent held his husband's hand tight as they navigated through the guests enjoying the poolside reception. *His husband.* Thinking those two words was like swallowing a rainbow. It filled him with light and love and most of all, promise. The promise of a lifetime of love and companionship with a man who made his blood run hot with a single touch. A man whose heart was as beautiful as the outside packaging. Growing up in a military household, he'd always sworn he wouldn't fall in love with a soldier, and he hadn't. He'd fallen for a Marine! His brothers gave him a lot of shit about his choice in men, but they did it out of love.

Rick lived the Marine Corps motto—*Semper Fidelis*—always faithful—in his civilian life. Anyone who knew him knew that about him, so Brent wasn't surprised in the least when the love of his life steered them toward his Marine buddy, and former lover, who was carrying on a conversation with Hank Travis, one of Jake's oldest friends and the drummer for BlackWing. The world renowned rock band had recently returned from an extended tour to promote their latest album, and the man knew how to tell a good story. A small crowd had gathered to listen.

"You don't mind, do you?" Rick asked.

"No, but do you think you'll be able to pull him away from Hank?"

"Won't know until I try." He squeezed Brent's hand. "Why don't you see if you can find Kenn? I'll drag Dave away if I have to then we can all meet up at the bar in a few."

He returned the hand squeeze adding a little tug. "I don't want to let go of you."

Rick thumbed the titanium band on Brent's ring finger. "We have the rest of our lives, baby. We can spare a few minutes to introduce our guys, can't we? I think they'll be good together."

"Or they'll hate each other then they'll hate us."

"Nah." His husband bent to place a gentle kiss on his lips. "Run along, now. Find Kenn and convince him he needs a beer. I'll get Dave."

Brent sighed and wrapped his arms around his husband's waist. Rick's arms surrounded him with love. "When did you become a matchmaker?"

"When I met you and realized what I'd been missing." His next kiss was more than a peck and a smidge less than an invitation to get naked. "I love you. I never knew true happiness until I met you. It hurts me to see Kenn and Dave alone. They're good men. They deserve to find their happy ever after."

"Like you found yours?"

His lips brushed lightly over Brent's. "Like *we* found *ours*." Brent's lips parted—an invitation Rick took advantage of. His mouth plundered. His tongue thrust in and out, mimicking the thrust and parry of their lower bodies. He didn't know how long they'd been locked in a carnal embrace when someone clapped him on the shoulder.

"Save that for the honeymoon, would ya?" His oldest brother, Bryce, the motherfucker.

Brent dropped his forehead to Rick's shoulder which shook with laughter. "Not funny. They're all looking at us, aren't they?"

"Pretty much," Rick confirmed. "Why don't we say the hell with our exes and get the fuck out of here?"

They'd long since cut the cake and listened to the requisite speeches. They'd only been hanging around out of courtesy, but fuck courtesy. "I think that's an excellent idea."

"Show's over, folks." Rick held him tight as he addressed the crowd. "Thanks for coming, now if you'll give us a minute to change out of these monkey suits, we'll be out to say goodbye."

Brent's cheeks were on fire as they made their way to the pool house. Once the door was locked behind them and Rick made sure the drapes were closed, it took only a minute for them to shed their wedding finery and come together heated flesh to heated flesh.

"They'll know," Brent cautioned.

"Do you care? Because I don't." Rick closed a hand around Brent's dick. "I'll never make it to the hotel. I need to be inside you. Now." They'd booked the honeymoon suite at one of Dallas's most prestigious hotels for the weekend. Monday, they'd fly to Alaska for a two-week outdoor adventure with a side of luxury accommodations Brent had insisted on as payment for camping on his honeymoon.

At Rick's touch, Brent's heart raced. He'd follow this man, *his husband*, to the ends of the earth. He palmed Rick's erection. God, he'd never get enough of him. He slid his free hand to the back of Rick's neck and pulled him in until their lips were almost touching. "Are you forgetting what today is?"

"If you're asking if I've forgotten the promise I made to you when I asked you to marry me, the answer is no. I haven't forgotten."

Brent stroked Rick's cock. "I held up my end of the bargain. I married you. You're mine, Rick. Forever and always. And I want what's mine."

Rick cradled his head in both hands, tilted his head so he could nibble on his earlobe. "I thought you'd rather wait until we got to the hotel so you could take your time."

Brent stroked Rick's cock harder. Damn, the man knew how to get his way, but he wasn't going to get it this time. "I've waited two years to make you mine. I'm not waiting a second longer. You aren't going to renege on our deal, are you, Marine?"

"No."

~ ~ ~

Brent pressed his lips to Rick's in a tender kiss that quickly burst into flames. Lips melded together; Brent walked him backward until his calves met the sofa then, hand on his chest, pushed him to his back on the plush cushions.

He'd really hoped Brent would forget about the deal they'd made or at least wait until they were somewhere more private, but the determination on his groom's face suggested the time for negotiations was over. He'd given Brent everything, except this one thing. He'd held back his submission, at first for selfish reasons, but as time went on, his motivations had changed. They'd done everything together but this, and he'd wanted to keep it that way until their wedding night. He'd saved his ass as a wedding present for Brent. Giving it to him now would have more meaning than anything else he could give him. It would mean more than the words they'd exchanged, the love they'd publicly declared, the rings they'd given each other. Submitting to Brent was the ultimate expression of his love for the man. If he wanted to claim his gift now, Rick wouldn't argue. "Wouldn't this be easier if I'm on my hands and knees?"

Brent shook his head. "I want to see your face when I shove my dick in you for the first time. I want to see your face when I make you mine."

Rick smiled to himself. *Right answer.* He wanted to see Brent's face, too. Wanted him to see the love, the trust in his eyes. "Whatever you want," he said, meaning every word. "There should be lube in the drawer over there." He pointed to an end table. If he knew his brother, there'd be lube and condoms in every room of the little love shack he fondly called a pool house.

"Remind me to thank Jake." Brent held up a small squeeze bottle.

"Over my dead body," he growled. The last thing he needed was Jake knowing for certain what they'd done in his guest accommodations. "This is none of his business."

Brent knelt on the sofa between Rick's legs. "Everyone is going to know anyway."

"Why do you say that?" He gripped his thighs and brought his knees up to his chest, his legs spread wide in invitation.

He squirted a generous amount of lube between Rick's cheeks. "Because I'm going to fuck you so damn hard, you'll need help walking out of here."

Rick groaned at his husband's declaration accompanied by two fingers spreading the cold liquid around his hole. It had been nearly three years since he'd allowed anyone the kind of intimacy he was granting Brent today, and he was loathe to admit he needed it every bit as much as Brent did. "Fuck, that feels good."

He applied more lube, working it inside with one finger, then another, stretching him a little at a time. "I've wanted to fuck you for so long, baby. I'm not going to last long."

"I don't care." He bucked his hips, silently begging for more. "We've got the rest of our lives, B., so quit fucking around and just do it."

"Someone's impatient."

Rick groaned at the teasing tone in his voice. Propping one leg up on the back of the sofa, he grabbed his dick and stroked. He was so fucking hard, he hurt. "Much more of that, and I'm going to blow without you. Is that what you want?"

Brent withdrew his fingers, making Rick moan and his hips rise…seeking. "Are you ready for me?"

He'd been ready for what seemed like forever. Taking Brent inside his body would be the final commitment between them. They'd truly belong to each other, partners for life. Taking Brent's cock in hand, he guided the head to his entrance. "Always ready, baby. Always."

Brent braced himself with one hand on the back of the sofa while the other cradled the back of Rick's neck, supporting him so he could watch their joining. "Watch, baby. Watch me claim what's mine." He flexed his hips and ever so slowly pushed his way in. Balls deep, his dick pulsing against Rick's walls. He held perfectly still, his gaze fixed on the point of their joining. Rick's rigid cock twitched. A bead of precum glistened on the tip.

"Fuuuck." Rick sucked in a breath and let it out. "Fuck, Brent. You feel so fuckin' good."

"I know." His husband's chest heaved above him. "You're so fucking beautiful. So fucking hot. I want to stay like this forever. Just you and me. Tell the rest of the world to go fuck themselves. Look at me."

Rick forced his gaze away from the miracle of their joining. Brent's eyes blazed with need, and an emotion deeper than anything Rick had ever experienced before. "I fucking love you, Rick Ingram. Now and forever. Your ass is mine. You're mine."

Rick swallowed hard. If he'd had any doubts about saving this part of himself for this moment, Brent's words and the emotion behind them, vanquished them. He'd done the right thing.

He dropped his arms, his hands on the cushion above his head in total surrender. "I love you, Brent Ingram. Everything I am belongs to you. I'm yours, now and forever."

Brent slowly withdrew then tunneled back in. Over and over as they gazed into each other's eyes, expressing their love in the most primal and physical way possible. Brent came first, emptying himself into Rick's tight channel. Afterward, he withdrew then took Rick into his mouth, ultimately taking the only gift he had left to give.

ABOUT THE AUTHOR

USA Today Best-Selling author Roz Lee is the author of over thirty romances. The first, The Lust Boat, was born of an idea acquired while on a Caribbean cruise with her family, and soon blossomed into a five-book series originally published by Red Sage. Following her love of baseball, Roz turned her attention to sexy athletes in tight pants, writing the critically acclaimed Mustangs Baseball series.

Roz has been married to her best friend, and high school sweetheart, for over four decades. They have two daughters and are the proud grandparents of three adorable grandkids. Roz and her husband live in the wilds of New Jersey with their Labrador Retriever, Bud which is code for Big Unruly Dog.

Even though Roz has lived on both coasts, her heart lies in between, in Texas. A Texan by birth, she can trace her family back to the Republic of Texas. With roots that deep, she says, "You can't ever really leave."

When Roz isn't writing, she's reading or traipsing around the country on one adventure or another. No trip is too small, no tourist trap too cheesy, and no road unworthy of travel.

Learn more at WWW.RozLee.net

www.ingramcontent.com/pod-product-compliance
Lightning Source LLC
Chambersburg PA
CBHW070418310726
48977CB00003B/743